BLUE EYED MOON

Legendary Stars Saga Book Three

Dai'Ja S. Rose

Nova Ink Books

BLUE EYED MOON

LEGENDARY STARS SAGA BOOK THREE

DAI'JA S. ROSE

NOVA INK BOOKS

Contact info: www.daijasrosebooks.com

ISBN (digital): 979-8-9891572-4-2

ISBN (paperback): 979-8-9891572-5-9

Edited by Susan Michaud

Map designed by: Luis Leopardi – Fiverr (leidolfr)

Nova Ink Books

To all of you experiencing your own metamorphosis – it's beautiful on the other side.

Kashmala

Wyndhm

Snow Trib

Beach Tribe

Jungle Tribe

Lower Ember

Upper Ember

Kindle

THEYRA

PYROC

Mystic Ocean

BOOKTOK PRAISE

"This book was a breath of fresh air for fantasy readers. I'm excited to read more of the Legends story!" – @mblazer21

"Prepare to be captivated by this debut fantasy novel brimming with enchanting magic and extraordinary characters. Eagerly awaiting the sequel." – @bookswithambs

"Jai's character had me hooked from the very beginning! Navigating his impossible fate and accepting the reality of his new found purpose was an exhilarating journey. This is one for those who struggle to find intention and those ever faced with a life or death choice. " – @bookbehavior

"The Golden Eyed Legend is a riveting new fantasy series that I simply could not put down!" – @laurenslibraryyy

"Fun, adventurous, and fiery. It was a fast-paced, action pack. Our story is set in a world where some have lost their magic and others have kept and nurtured it. The story centers on a young man named Jai who was orphaned and taken in at a young age. One day he finds out he was gifted with a great power and must begin his adventure to control and protect his new found family and friends. I will say it is a nice debut. It is fast paced and to the point. Which I am always a fan of. It is also heavily ATLA inspired and I am loving the opportunity to jump into a similar world with fun and powerful characters all trying to move forward and discover themselves and their goals." – @theladyravens

"Golden Eyed Legend is the perfect book for a fantasy lover, and the perfect book if you don't know fantasy or are new to it. I love the world building and the characters arcs. Calida was my favorite! I love a strong willed woman! This book gave me Avatar the Last Airbender vibes in the best way! It was action packed and hard to put down as you wanted to continually know what happened next. For a debut novel, especially in fantasy, I can say this checks all the boxes, amazing world building, likeable characters, great buildup and character arcs and an ability to keep you engaged from the very first chapter. If I had to use one word to describe this book it would be impactful, you feel something from every character and it adds to the story."

– @paristhebibliophile

"I really enjoyed reading this. It's not the typical genre I would normally read, but after reading this it's something I'm interested in reading more! I thought the description, the imagery, and the flow of the book was spectacular. It's very well written for a first time writer! I can't wait to read more from you in the future." – @cheyennetatikaaa

"The world building in the Golden Eyed Legend is intricate and intriguing. I found the magic system unique and an immediate draw. Instantly, I was curious about Jai's backstory and wanted to know more. If you're looking for the next epic fantasy read, this is it!" – @dmcancel

** @dmcancel is the author of *Blood & Sunlight* and *Shadows & Secrets*

Water is renewal. Where there is water, there is life.
Water is transformation, it seeks change and movement.
There is clarity in moving forward. Likewise, there is growth
in change.
If one is not growing, they are ultimately dying.
So do not fear change.
Even the moon changes in cycles. You rise with the moon,
embracing its beauty and tranquility.
One who bears water wields power in the serene.

BLOOD | HANDS | EQUALITY

G reat Heavens,

Oh, grand skies, what have I done? You blessed me in abundance, and I took your blessings for granted. I am truly sorry for the pain and hatred that I have caused. I disobeyed your laws, which were established for our protection. As a result, no one is safe now. I never believed that one person could change the plight of many people. I apologize for the chaos my life and death caused. I betrayed, and then I was betrayed, and rightfully so. The aftermath of the problems I failed to solve will plague my people for generations. Never before did I own my contributions to this mess of a world, but now I must.

Please let her place a mighty value on family. This is something I did not do. As a result, I never knew any of my children. I will never touch their lives in any way. Heavens, grant her family and make her cleave to it. Open her heart to fight and sacrifice for what will benefit her people. Make her nothing like me—selfish and without remorse. Let her heart experience every emotion deeply, yet not one emotion too much. May her heart and unyielding love guide her stars. May her love be as pure as the clearest water.

Great Universe, forgive me. I have torn down much. If it be your will, may the people remember my good works too. I am not worthy of their praises, but may they know I tried? I lived as a man who made many mistakes and tried to fix what I could. I was loved and did a lousy job of showing love in return. Cyra, Avala, Soleil, Selene, and Janara, I am truly sorry.

I did not love you enough. My successor, I am not sure what lies in the wake of my death, but I know it will be nothing less than chaos. For the pain and suffering you are bound to endure, I apologize. For what lies in my wake, Heavens, I pray, let her save them.

    -Aenon

CHAPTER 1

N avy eyes flashed open. No longer in the snow, Tiber struggled to raise her head.

Where? How?

Her vision was hazy. However, she could hear voices. She groaned. Her body was not in pain, but her head was throbbing terribly. After taking a few deep breaths, she tried to recall how she ended up in this unfamiliar place. Flickers of memory began to emerge, but they were fragmented and incomplete. After several moments of utter confusion, she suddenly remembered her confrontation with the Windmaster Seer. Shocked that she was even alive, Tiber remembered the fury in

Aqila's eyes, the storm she raged, and the incredible power that she possessed.

Those startling silver eyes threatened to be her undoing. Tiber's hands slowly touched her throat. She felt her airways constricting. She trembled to think how close she came to suffocation. Aqila, the deadly beauty, was a Storm—a Windmaster whose nature was not attuned to peace but chaos. Tiber would rather die than ever see those piercing silver eyes again.

A part of her still refused to believe that the last two days' events were real. A steady feeling of dread began to consume Tiber. She failed her mission. Not only did she not gather any information on Jai, but she also knew Nahal would not spare Neptune any details of the degree of her failure. She had come so close. How did things go so wrong? Fluttering her eyes briefly, she saw a face peering down at her. She sat up quickly—a little too quick.

"Take it easy. I'm here. I am relieved Muraco and Shasa found you when they did." A man with deep blue eyes and dark brown hair embraced her.

Father?

"Muraco and Shasa?"

"Yes, my girl." He squeezed her so tight she could barely breathe. The sensation was too much for Tiber; it reminded her of Aqila.

Pushing her father away slightly, she whispered, "I'm okay." Then Tiber buried her face into her father's neck, trying not to cry.

"What happened? Who attacked our tribesmen?"

Tiber's eyes went wide. She couldn't tell her father about her ventures. Her father would never approve, and if he knew about the Seer, she would be in deep trouble. "Nahal and I found them there, and then I got knocked out. It happened so quickly. I don't remember seeing anything," she lied.

Her father cupped her round, chestnut face, "I will find who did this and make them pay." He quickly stood to his feet, adjusting his heavy black parka before exiting the icy cave. Tiber realized that she was in the medicine lair. Nahal was several feet away from her, still unconscious. She was puzzled about what could have happened to the tribesmen. Aqila didn't do anything to them unless she finished them off after choking her to the point of unconsciousness. But something didn't seem right. How could she have taken on the tribesmen when she was considerably outnumbered? She was powerful, but could she have been that powerful? Was Aqila a Seer at all? Was she something greater? Was she a L—

"Tiber, love, you're awake." A tan-skinned woman rushed toward her. Her dark blue eyes glistened with concern. She lightly cradled her stomach before sitting beside Tiber.

"I'm fine, Shasa, and you should be taking it easy."

"I was so worried about you. Muraco and I decided to go walking so I could get some exercise, and our hearts stopped when we saw you and Nahal. Muraco was worried you two might have had a fight or something until we noticed our tribesmen. What happened?"

"I don't know. Nahal and I found them like that, and someone knocked me out. I'm just sorry that I didn't see anything."

"I'm glad that you are all right, love. My world would end if something happened to you. I can't believe someone would attack us like that first thing in the morning. These past couple of weeks have been so stressful." Shasa rubbed her small, barely noticeable bump.

"Wait! Weeks? How long have I been here?"

"Two weeks," Shasa gently answered before stroking Tiber's hair. She focused on the welcomed sensation of Shasa running her fingers through her hair in a gentle, comforting motion. Tiber felt her tangles release as a warm wave of peace enveloped her.

With each stroke of her hand, Shasa could feel the knots and worries melting from her younger sister's mind. She kept her touch light and soothing, knowing that her sibling needed nothing more than to feel her love and protection. "What's the matter? You seem uneasy."

"I guess I'm still shaken about everything." Tiber trembled.

"Father will protect us. He always has. We will get to the bottom of this, I promise."

I'm at the bottom of this.

Tiber felt like she was about to have a heart attack. She couldn't catch her breath. Neptune would be furious with her, and if she angered him, he wouldn't save Shasa.

How could I have gambled with my sister's life like that?

"Tiber? Tiber?" Shasa called over the healer.

"It's okay, Tiber. Take deep breaths. In and out—that's right. Shasa, I'm afraid something took her by surprise. She needs to rest now. I'll look after her," the steel-blue-eyed young woman spoke.

Shasa stood and gently touched the healer's beautiful, ebony-hued skin, "Thank you, Sita, but if there is any way that I can help, let me know." Shasa sighed before slowly walking away.

"Thanks, Sita," Tiber murmured.

"Of course. Now, continue with the deep breathing exercises. Are you okay? You seem so stressed. Was the conversation with Shasa a little too much?"

"I'll be okay. Maybe my talk with my sister was a little much." Tiber sighed.

"Well, your father wants to hold a tribe meeting once Nahal awakens."

"Oh, a tribe meeting about what?"

"I don't have any details, silly. However, the meeting won't be far off. Nahal has been stirring all day. He may awaken soon. Just rest up for now, okay?"

Tiber watched Sita walk away to tend to the multiple injured tribesmen. It was fascinating watching her work with so much care and attention. She always admired her tribe sister. Sita was a couple of years older than her, but her wits and maturity were something to marvel over. At least twenty people were being tended to, and Sita was as calm as possible. She had everyone patched up on their icy beds in an orderly fashion. If the healer was overwhelmed, she never let it show. On the other hand, Tiber had a dreadful feeling about her future.

Will Neptune come looking for me? Will he still help Shasa?

She sighed. The most important thing was that no one discovered what really happened. If her father finds out that she captured and attacked the Seer, he would be furious. That would be considered an act of war, and her tribe could exile her. Also, he must never know that she is working for Neptune. Many Waterbearers regard Neptune as a leader; others, like Nahal, believed Neptune was a god in human form. Some believed he should have sole control of all Waterbearer tribes. Her father disagreed with this line of thinking. He was a firm believer in the tradition that each tribe should have its own sovereign land and its own chief and council. Her father would feel dishonored knowing his daughter was working for someone who could potentially rob him of his position.

Tiber thought about what she would say at the meeting should the topic be discussed. She and Nahal would have to conceal the truth about their dealings. She wondered how much the tribesmen would remember about Aqila. If they said they saw Aqila, the tribe might make a move against the Windmasters. Although, when the Windmasters had last been at war with the Landkeepers, they were victorious. If they had any soldiers half as strong as Aqila, the small tribe of Snow and Ice would be in great trouble.

Coughing disturbed her train of thought. Sita turned to Nahal. "You're awake! Take it easy now. It seems like you had some poison in your system. I have never seen anything like that before. Sorry it took so long."

Nahal slowly sat up, groaning. He blinked slowly before running his long, slender fingers through his hair. His gaze seemed lost.

Sita walked over and gently massaged his shoulders. "How are you feeling? I'll admit, it took a while to remedy the poison."

"I appreciate all you did to ensure I survived, and that's what matters now. Sita, I hate to inconvenience you more than I already have, but I have a specific tea in my tent that would help me relax. Would you get it for me?"

"I would, but I don't think I should be going to your tent." Sita averted her gaze. She sighed, "I guess I can ask your brother Muraco. I'll be back."

Sita hurried out of the medicine lair, leaving Tiber and Nahal as the only ones conscious.

After several minutes, Tiber hissed, "That was awful, making Sita feel all uncomfortable and awkward like that after she saved your life."

"My life wouldn't have needed saving if you weren't a traitor to the cause," he spat.

"Nahal, I did not betray you. The Seer had to have been a Storm or something, and that was probably why she was able to escape."

"A Storm? Hmm. Wild, raging power ran through her veins. You might be onto something. Despite the lethal amount of poison in her system, she did the impossible. Still, Neptune will be furious to hear this. And with these tribesmen like this, your father will probably want to have a meeting."

"It's already scheduled. He was just waiting for you to wake up."

"Hmm, is that so? How long have I been out?"

"Shasa said two weeks. I woke a little before you," Tiber explained.

"Two weeks! Icy hell! Neptune probably already knows that we failed. Tiber, no one can find out about this."

"I know. Just follow my lead."

"Your lead? Did you forget you got us into this mess? You captured the Seer and poisoned her."

"Yeah? You violently attacked her until she fought back, and the other tribesmen had to suffer."

"The other tribesmen were part of Neptune's alliance to provide cover for you to bring back the Legend. I had nothing to do with what happened to them. We don't even know what happened. We would have seen or heard something if someone else was there. So the Seer had to have attacked them to escape. Besides, I wouldn't have had to attack her if she wasn't here, now, would I?"

"Just work with me. We're like brother and sister. We really need to work together."

"I'm back," Sita called, holding a small herbal packet in her hand. I told Muraco and Chief Dalit that both of you were awake. They are preparing for a meeting in a few minutes."

"You told my brother?"

"And my father?" Tiber questioned.

I haven't thought of anything to say.

"I had to tell Muraco so I could go into Nahal's tent. It would have been improper not to, and I don't want anyone getting the wrong idea. You know how that would have looked to be a single woman entering the tent of a single man. Muraco told your father, Tiber. They seem anxious to have this meeting. They are calling the tribe to gather now. Nahal, I will make your tea once the meeting is over. You have my word."

"Of course." Nahal rubbed his temples.

Tiber fell silent for several minutes while Nahal talked to Sita. He didn't seem bothered by the prospect of being questioned about what happened two weeks ago. Tiber was nervous as icy hell and worried about the consequences, and Nahal was acting like there was nothing wrong. Tiber turned to the cave entrance and saw Mika approaching; she purred when Tiber petted her beautiful spotted head.

The loud beating of drums echoed throughout the medicine lair, piercing the air with its melodic rhythm.

"I guess it's time for the meeting," Sita murmured.

Tiber slowly mounted her snow leopard. "Sita, are you coming?"

The steel-blue-eyed girl nodded. With that, Tiber left riding Mika up the mountain to the meeting cave. It was packed, which was unusual. There was a pit in her stomach at the thought of speaking in front of the entire tribe. Her father wore his black feather headdress and sat on a solid ice chair adorned with a beaded yak pelt.

Her father, the chief, motioned for Tiber to come up to the front. Her feet trembled in her boots. Every step felt weighed as she dragged toward the front. She felt self-conscious as various shades of blue eyes watched her approach the front of the cave. Right as she stood beside her father, Nahal and Sita entered.

"Nahal, join us up here, my son," Chief Dalit called, motioning him forward.

Tiber wished she were like Nahal. He was smooth, smart, and confident. His body language exuded superiority, and his footsteps were assertive. Nahal had the respect of everyone in the tribe, and with his dangerous charm, it was not unusual for him to capture the attention of the young women.

How does he do that?

As Nahal stood opposite Tiber, the chief continued, "The Tribe of Snow and Ice has survived a malicious attack on our people. Nahal, Tiber, focus and tell us what you can about that morning. Anything you remember will be useful. Once we have the details, our tribe will prepare for retaliation."

Tiber cleared her throat. "That morning, Nahal and I heard noises near the river. Together we went to investigate. As we got closer, we noticed some of our tribesmen lying unconscious. Then I was knocked unconscious."

The chief raised his eyebrows. "All right, Nahal. Do you have anything to add to this account?"

"Yes, my Chief, I do. Tribe of Snow and Ice, Tiber captured and poisoned the Seer. She brought her back to the cave where I confronted her. The Seer was sick from the poison, and I questioned Tiber's judgment. She expressed interest in making an exchange of some kind, gambling with the Seer's life. As I continued to try to reason with her, the Seer, who was also a Storm, overcame the poison. In a state of alarm, this female Windmaster was in self-defense mode. She was summoning an unbelievable power as a last resort to save herself. I do not know the details of what happened to the tribesmen, as I never saw them. Tiber eventually tried to help me calm the Seer. Then Tiber had a change of heart and continued to attack the Windmaster until neither of us was conscious. And that is the truth."

Everyone fell silent; Tiber's eyes widened, and her body began trembling violently. She couldn't breathe.

What the icy hell, Nahal! What are you trying to do?

"Nahal! What?"

"I'm sorry, Tiber, I had to tell them the truth."

Chief Dalit stood looking from Tiber to Nahal. He placed his hand across Mika's pelt before speaking, "Elder Akay, you know the truth from a lie. Which of these young people spoke the truth, and who spoke a lie?"

An elderly woman slowly walked forward. Her baby blue eyes were blind and lackluster. "My good Chief, Mahak's boy spoke the truth, and your daughter gave us a lie."

Everyone gasped.

Murmurs rang through the icy cave.

"Tiber lied?"

"She was always such a sweet girl!"

"Why would she capture a Seer?"

"This could start a war! What was she thinking?"

"There's no way we would survive against Kashmala and Wyndhm!"

Tiber's throat felt tight as she fought back tears. "Father, please!"

"Tiber, my girl," he hung his head in disappointment. "Send her to the Cave of Shame."

"Father, I beg you! Please, don't—" That was all Tiber could say before all went black before her eyes.

CHAPTER 2

When Tiber woke up, it was no longer early evening but nighttime in Avala. The back of her head was throbbing. She reached back and felt a knot. There was a searing pain whenever she touched it. She began to groan, and a small hand covered her mouth. When Tiber turned, she saw Sita covering her mouth.

"There's a guard outside. You don't want him to know that you're awake."

"Why is there a guard outside your medicine lair," Tiber whispered.

"They hit you too hard, and I insisted I look at the injury. Tiber, what is going on? Why did you lie?" Sita shook Tiber's shoulders violently.

"I'm so sorry! Sita, I've gotten myself into some trouble. Yes, I lied, but Nahal did too. He was with me all the way. The Seer had been with us for a whole day before the incident. Nahal even went to try and retrieve an antidote after I poisoned her. I did intend to capture her, but I didn't mean to put her life in danger. There is more to the story than what Nahal let on," Tiber frantically explained.

Sita lowered her head. "I know he lied. I could tell . . ."

Tiber's blue eyes went wide. "Sita, that would mean that—"

"It just started happening. So I can only do it when the moon is full, half, or new. That's why I have to be careful. Nahal mostly told the truth. He would tell a true statement and skip to another true statement, and that's how he was able to cover it. There were so many gaps in his account. After you passed out, Elder Akay suggested that we question Nahal again so she could confirm the apparent gaps in his story . . . I guess she could tell as well. She tried to explain that she wanted to hear more of Nahal's account, but the tribe was in shock to hear that you lied. Nahal conveniently passed out at that point. Muraco took him to his tent. Tiber, what will you do?"

"Sita, I made a mistake in capturing the Seer, and right now, she's the only one who can clear my name. I must find her, and I will return once I do. Sita, this is something that I can only tell you. Over the past year, Nahal and I have been working for Neptune. Nahal will not stop serving him. I need you to help me. Something is going on, please, Sita," Tiber pleaded with her young friend for assistance.

"So Neptune is real?"

Tiber nodded.

"I will help you, but I have conditions: we meet near the border of the Jungle tribe to keep me updated, and you must disassociate with Neptune. You're worried about what he will do to you. That should be a sign that something is wrong. I will get close to Nahal and try to get what I can, but I'm not going to help you get out of this if you plan to go back to Neptune. I know why you lied, but you must stop. People are going to get hurt. Technically, the Windmasters could charge us with an act of war. If they do, they will obliterate us," Sita explained.

"I understand, and I agree to your conditions. Don't send me to the Cave of Shame. Let me slip out, speak to my father, and escape. I will meet you every two weeks on the border we share with the Jungle tribe."

"All right, just be ready." Sita stood in the darkness and walked to the guard outside.

He turned to her. "Is everything all right, Sita?"

She sighed, "Actually, I don't feel well. It's been a stressful two weeks. All the tribesmen's injuries and now this with Tiber, I'm just feeling weak." Sita wobbled and collapsed to her knees.

"Sita!" The guard caught her. "Let me take you to your tent. You need some rest."

The guard carried Sita bridal-style away from the medicine lair.

Tiber crept up and rushed away from the lair as fast as her legs would take her. Mika was lying near the edge of the ice cliff. She perked up as she noticed her master. Tiber hurried to her father's tent. Once inside, she called out to him. He staggered from one of his rooms, panting heavily.

"Are you okay, Father?"

"Tiber, you have to go." He clutched his chest as he fell to his knees.

Oblivious to the situation, words poured from her mouth. "I'm sorry I lied, but Nahal's account was not all to the story. I mean, yes, I did poison and capture the Seer, and it was my fault she attacked. But there was a lot more to what happened." Tiber tried to help her father up, pulling on his brown hands. He was too heavy and too tired to move.

"I sent you to the cave to protect you. Tiber, you must go. Take Mika, never leave her behind."

"I'm so sorry, Father," Tiber's eyes watered.

"I know everything, my love. Betrayal runs deep. Save this tribe. Tiber, save this tribe." He began to cough up blood.

"Father!" Crouching beside him, Tiber wiped the blood away with her sleeve and tried to prop her father's head. His breath became ragged, then none at all. Tiber tried to stifle her sobs. "Daddy, wake up! Don't leave me, Daddy, please."

"Traitor and a murderer." Nahal gasped as he entered the tent.

"Nahal, it's not what it seems," Tiber pleaded, her eyes glazed with a layer of tears.

"You know, the more you say that, the less I believe it. Guards! Tiber killed her father! Chief Dalit is dead!"

There was a ruckus in the tribe. The thunder of footsteps resounded in their direction. Tiber reluctantly let her father go and ran to the back of his tent. Nahal was right behind her. He summoned sharp shards of ice at her, attempting to slow her down. She blasted him backward with a harsh spurt of water. He tripped!

As Tiber hastily exited the tent, Mika rushed to her. She mounted the big cat and ran from Avala. Tiber saw a rush of tribesmen. Mika instinctively ran faster to get away. Then it happened, Mika cried out and collapsed. She looked back to see Nahal with a crossbow. Her father's crossbow! He shot Mika in the side. He readied the bow again, hitting the cat in its side again. Mika was profusely bleeding.

"Mika, please hang on. Mika!"

Nahal and the tribesmen steadily came closer, spears and crossbows readied, trying to surround the chief's daughter. With tears flooding her eyes, she only knew one thing: she would not die tonight. She used her ability to break the icy cliff off the mountain, plummeting her and her cat into the icy river.

Nahal growled, "Let's go! Follow them!"

"No, son, look at your tribesmen. Several men are down. You hardly have anyone to go after her. Our chief is dead. Let's put the priority in the right place. We will track Tiber later. Tribe of Snow and Ice, let's prepare the chief for burial. Shasa, did your father communicate with you about a successor?" asked a tall man who looked to be in his thirties with deep mahogany skin and bold, sharp cerulean eyes. He was obviously much older, but he hardly appeared to be aging.

"No sir, he told me he had a written decree about who the successor will be. I wish I knew where it was, Mahak," Shasa said in between sobs.

"Father! This is not the time to interrogate my wife!" Muraco stepped in front of Shasa, shielding her from the eyes of their tribe.

"Muraco, don't be so emotional, it was a simple question. Tribe, as per our customs, we will reconvene to vote on a temporary chief until the decree has been located," Mahak suggested.

"Father, that sounds fair, but as you said, we should bury the chief first," Muraco replied.

Mahak whispered to Muraco, "I know this is hard for everyone, especially Shasa. Don't let your emotions blind you. Your wife needs your understanding, but she also needs your strength. Don't let her see you as weak and emotional. Trust me, we will endure."

Muraco nodded in respect. "Wise words, Father."

Mahak sighed, "Dalit was the chief and Shasa's father, but he was my best friend. I've known him for a lifetime. Please don't think I'm void of pain; I just wear it as a man. You must do the same."

The tribe began to disperse, and Muraco and Shasa lingered behind. His cerulean eyes gently gazed into her dark blue eyes, "I am so sorry about your father. It will be okay, Shasa." He gently touched her baby bump.

"Muraco, I don't believe Tiber killed our father. I won't believe it unless she swears to it herself! She loved Father and he loved her. I don't know what's going on. I can't protect her."

"Shh, it will be okay. Something is going on around here. Listen to me. We aren't going to make any bold moves, and we will lie low. Your father has been telling us of his suspicions. We need to be careful."

"How can I not blame myself for this? I don't know what I missed! What did I do to make her distant? We never kept secrets from each other. She's a good girl! She's never lied to me."

"Shasa, it's not your fault, Tiber's an adult making her own choices, mistakes will happen."

"No, she is not an adult. She still has the body of a child! She needs me!"

"She will be okay. Tiber's getting older and finding herself and she's bound to make mistakes—it's normal. We will be here doing everything we can to help." He wiped her eyes dry, and the couple proceeded to follow the tribe.

CHAPTER 3

Nahal walked into Sita's tent, where the guard was. "So the chief's death doesn't bother you, Chelan?"

The blue-eyed guard turned around. "Chief's death? What? What happened? I didn't hear you call out! Nahal, Sita fell ill. I brought her back to her tent. We are on the other side of the tribe's land. If I had heard you call, I would have been the first to respond. You know me! Please, forgive me." Chelan lowered his head.

Upon hearing Nahal enter, Sita slightly opened her eyes. She meant to buy Tiber time. She did not intend to get Chelan in trouble. Sita kept still as she feigned sleep.

"You're the lead warrior. Not a good look. The tribe's safety is in your hands, and you fumbled."

"I made a grave mistake; forgive me, brother."

Nahal considered Chelan's words and opened his arms in a brotherly embrace. Chelan accepted. As soon as Nahal let go, he punched Chelan under the chin, immediately rendering him unconscious. The loud thud of Chelan's body hitting the floor nearly made Sita jump.

Nahal sighed. "That's your problem. You trust too easily." He walked over to Sita and looked at her closely. "Tiber probably got into something to make Sita sick so she could get away. I never thought she could be capable of such treason." He turned on his heels and yelled from the tent door, "Tribesmen, come over here! Come over here!"

The remaining men rushed over at Nahal's call. "Brothers, this is where your lead warrior is. This is unacceptable! Wasn't he supposed to be watching Tiber? He must be punished in her place until she is found."

"Wait, Nahal! We should allow him to give an account with the Elder Akay present. Until then, we should keep him guarded," Muraco tried to reason with Nahal.

"Brother, in another situation, what you are saying would be ideal, but Tiber has murdered our chief. If Chelan were on his post, that would not have happened."

"That's true," a tribesman agreed.

"Chelan is the lead warrior; he knows better than to leave his post unattended."

"I guess it wouldn't hurt to try Nahal's way, given the situation," another tribesman replied.

"What's going on?" Sita sat up.

Nahal rushed to her side. "Sita, are you okay? Tiber has escaped, and she killed her father before she left."

Sita's eyes brimmed with tears. "What? Chief Dalit? He's dead?"

"Nahal, how insensitive of you to tell Sita like that." Muraco groaned at his brother.

Sita cried, hugging her knees.

Seeing her upset made Nahal uneasy. He sat beside her, gently pressing his chin on top of her head. "Shhh, it's okay. I'm sorry. I shouldn't have said it like that. Forgive me for being callous. Chelan neglected his post. I will remove him," Nahal reassured her. He wiped her tears from her eyes. He whispered in her ear, "I'm doing my best for the tribe, but I'll come back and make you some tea later tonight."

Nahal stood and headed to the entrance of Sita's tent. "Brothers, we should look for Tiber before she becomes a greater threat."

"After we give our chief a proper burial." Muraco eyed Nahal carefully.

"Of course, we wouldn't want to bring our chief dishonor through an inappropriate burial service," Nahal agreed with his older brother.

The tribesmen dispersed, and the two brothers were left looking each other in the eyes. "Nahal, I'm proud of you for taking charge like this," Muraco said, walking over and draping his arm around his younger brother's shoulder. "You are doing a great job. Just don't forget our customs. The tribe's customs have kept us alive for thousands of years despite being cursed."

"We must give all our brothers and sisters complete equality and show them unyielding fairness. I think we should not jump to conclusions about Tiber. She's a tribe sister, and we should ensure she receives equality too."

"You're right, brother. I'll keep that in mind. However, there still is a possibility that this was a premeditated attack. If so, Chelan and Tiber could be partners in a murder. But, brother, I will hold your words close to my heart."

Muraco nodded and followed the rest of the soldiers. Nahal looked back at Sita and left her tent, dragging Chelan's body behind him.

"I'll be back, okay? Take it easy."

Several moments passed before Sita felt like she could move. She was caught off guard and was left feeling afraid and guilty. She knew in her bones that Tiber would never kill her father. They were so close. But Tiber was in danger, and Chelan was in trouble because of her. Chelan would not have been out of position when the chief was killed if it wasn't for her. Her heart was racing. Her palms were sweating. She felt alone and lost, and the situation scared her. And she was puzzled by Nahal.

Why would he knock Chelan out? The chief was killed. Why would he want to have the lead guard out of position?

Her body felt cold in his absence. Despite being confused, she longed for Nahal's company.

"Permission to enter?"

"Come in," Sita said softly.

She smiled when Nahal entered. His demeanor was much calmer than before. He pulled his curls of dark brown hair into a small bun. His gaze was gentle yet still piercing.

"I promised to come back."

"I know. I don't want you breaking rules for me—we aren't supposed to be alone like this."

"I find that comment laced with just a touch of hypocrisy, seeing that Chelan was in here not too long ago." He smirked.

"And I wasn't awake to remind him of the rules."

"Fair enough." Nahal smirked as he heated a cup of water over a small fire pit in Sita's tent. He carefully added some tea leaves.

"Thank you," she whispered.

"It's the least I could do. I mean, you took care of us when we were unconscious. And I should not have been so harsh in delivering the news about the chief."

"Why did you hit him?"

"Ahh, Chelan? Hmm, you saw that? So you can see in your sleep now?"

"I was starting to wake up." Sita giggled at the funny expression Nahal was making.

"I was angry! I know I shouldn't have hit him. And I should not have made him look bad. But I was so upset! He has one job! If he was doing his one job, the chief may be alive. He deserves a punishment. This is not a light offense.

At the end of the day, I want the best for our tribe. I'm willing to do whatever it takes for that to happen."

"So am I." She met his gaze; goosebumps peppered her skin. She was glad it was cold and her parka covered her arms. "Why did you say what you said at the meeting? Elder Akay wanted to fill the gaps in your story. Are you trying to get Tiber in trouble?"

"No, but you heard the chief. He wanted to retaliate! The Windmasters would have wiped us out. We had no leg to stand on after Tiber poisoned their Seer. And she wasn't going to say what she did. If I went along with her story, we would have attacked them, and they would have ended us. I'm not saying I did everything perfectly. I couldn't let her sign a death wish for all of us."

"You were trying to protect us," she whispered.

"Here, drink up and try to relax. If you need anything, you know where to find me."

She froze as his cool fingers grazed hers when offering her the tea. Her brain forgot how to think. Her lips parted slightly as Nahal stood to leave. She never responded. Her voice didn't work. She watched him walk away from her. The warmth from his presence evaporated to nothing as her tent flap closed, leaving her utterly alone. Sita brought her lips to the cup and slowly drank her tea. It only served to melt her mind further as the masculine scent of pine that was Nahal lingered in the tent.

She shook her head violently, "What in icy hell am I thinking? Tiber! Tiber needs me!"

She wanted to believe that Nahal had a good reason for what he was doing.

Tiber said they were working with Neptune together, but why? Neptune has a murky reputation. He has done really good things and some absolutely horrendous things. There has to be a reason.

To help Tiber, Sita would need an ally. There was no way she could take all of this on by herself. It would not be wise to get Shasa involved, especially since she was pregnant. Maybe Chelan will help her. Sita thought long and hard. Chelan will help her because she can give him something he no longer has. Freedom.

*****

Tiber emerged from the icy river; her body was shaking with cold and adrenaline. By plunging into the frigid waters, hoping to escape the clutches of her pursuers, the water had taken her breath away. Rushing to get to safety, she stumbled out of the water and onto the snow-covered bank. Tiber struggled to catch her breath. Her clothes were soaked through, and the cold was beginning to seep into her bones, but she knew that she had to keep moving to get as far away from her tribe as possible. To the east was her home tribe, westward was the Jungle tribe, and across the icy sea, would be the Beach tribe. Tiber headed west. Exhaustion plagued her every step as she was covered in blood. Mika's breathing was ragged. Being plunged into the icy river did nothing to help her worsening condition. Using all the strength she could muster, Tiber desperately pulled the cat to the border her tribe shared with the Jungle tribe.

Although she wasn't sure if this was a good decision, her only other option was to flee to the Beach tribe. Their Chiefess, Marina, was known to be moody and play the center field between World Order and Universal Order. Her father taught her that a man with no clear alliance is more dangerous than a known enemy. Marina was a good woman at heart. There was no doubt about that. However, her emotional vulnerability made her unreliable.

With trembling hands dripping with Mika's blood, Tiber's eyes scanned the surrounding area for any signs of danger. She walked until the ground was no longer icy but just oversaturated. The trees changed, the temperature grew warmer, and the air was laden with humidity. She was getting close. The edge of the jungle was silent, and the only sounds were the rushing of the water and the beating of her own heart. She stayed close to the river to keep her bearings, her mind focused on one thing and one thing only: survival. Eventually, she saw some heavy brush that would provide cover for her and Mika.

After Tiber pulled Mika into the thick jungle brush, she went back to cover her tracks. She summoned wave behind wave of water until the icy shore showed no signs of disturbance. Another lesson her father taught her. She raced back to the jungle as fast as her tired legs could run. Mika's rough pants alarmed her. Pulling some leaves from the brush, she began to clean her loyal cat's wounds. Mika was too frail to hiss and groaned in pain at this point. The reality of everything hit Tiber violently. She began to sob. Maybe she should have gone to Marina. They were no different. She was just as emotionally vulnerable as the chiefess. What started as a noble venture ended in the loss of life and a pending war on her tribe's heels.

"What have I done?"

Tiber cried into Mika's gray spotted pelt. The lingering warmth was the only thing to comfort her right now. She looked up to the full moon. How the moon had been kind to her on this long night. Had it not been a full moon, Sita would not have recognized Nahal's lie.

How could the moon, which consumes life, save lives too? Was this what Aqila meant? Is this what it feels like to believe in the Universe? Is there something more for me beyond this? Is it possible for me to have a destiny too?

Tiber wiped her eyes as she applied pressure to Mika's wounds, slowing the bleeding. Her heart screamed for her father. In his last words to her, he said he knew everything. He told her to save her tribe and never leave Mika behind. Why would he trust her if he thought she betrayed his trust? Could she save her tribe? Could she even save Mika? Tiber gazed up to the moon while her cat began to sleep. For the first time, she realized how beautiful the moon was. Tonight, it was a shimmering white, the color of snow. Her throat felt tight from crying.

"Universe, I have never believed in you. Tonight, I am alone. Everything that I have known and loved is out of my reach. I have betrayed my family, yet I don't want to die. But more so, I don't want my sister to die. She is innocent, loving, and gentle. I would be satisfied with that ending if she lives and I die. Also, spare Mika. She was a gift from my father and Shasa. She has been with me for as long as I can remember. Spare her, even if for no reason other than that she's more loyal than me."

Aqila's words rang in her head: *when we repent with a true heart, the Universe forgives us.* Those words kept replaying in her mind. Would the Universe forgive her? Her eyes locked on the moon. She focused on its glow and presence. A wave of calm washed over her the longer she focused on it.

Suddenly, piercing pangs shot through her. It felt like her insides were burning. She wanted to cry out in pain but didn't dare risk it. Not with Nahal telling the tribe that she killed her father. The pain was centralized in her head and deep in her stomach. Tiber curled up in a fetal position, her face twisted in agony as she struggled with the intense pain coursing through her body. The cramps had come on suddenly and were unlike anything she had ever experienced. They felt like hot knives stabbing deep into her abdomen, and no matter how she shifted her position or tried to breathe through the pain, it only seemed to intensify.

Cramping, surging pain—she sat up, clutching her stomach. Then doubling over, she rocked, trying to hold onto some form of sanity. With each passing moment, she felt more and more helpless, as if the pain was consuming her whole being. Sweat broke out on her forehead, and her breath came in short, shallow gasps. It was as if her body had turned traitor, attacking her from the inside with a viciousness that left her reeling. Tiber had never experienced this kind of sensation. It seemed as if nothing she did could provide her any relief. Tears streamed down her face slowly as she tried to manage.

Hours passed, and her suffering continued. She didn't know what to make of what was happening. Tiber was tired, hurting, and hungry. For what felt like an eternity, she endured the cramps, her body wracked with spasms, and her mind consumed with pain. But gradually, as the intensity of the cramps began to ebb, she felt a glimmer of hope. With a deep breath, she steadied herself; instinct told her that she had survived the worst of it. Though the pain was still there, it was now manageable, and she knew that she would get through it, one agonizing moment at a time. Her eyes struggled to stay open. No, she wasn't comfortable, but sleep was becoming more of a necessity than a luxury. And at last, she could no longer deny herself; utterly exhausted, her eyes closed.

CHAPTER 4

Sita made a sleeping herb in her tent and poured it onto a cloth. She had to talk with Chelan alone. She changed from her everyday light blue fur pants to a dark blue pair and tied her waist-length, curly brown hair into a sloppy bun. Cautiously, she left her tent. After approaching the Cave of Shame from the back, she peered at the guard's position. He was pacing back and forth. Sita felt terrible for him. Being down so many men from the attack, he would not be relieved from duty. He was tired. Pacing was the only thing he could do to keep himself awake.

When his back was turned, she rushed behind him, covering his face with the cloth. She pulled him into a sitting position and leaned his head back slightly on the cave rock. At first glance, no one would think he was asleep. Sita hurried into the Cave of Shame. It was dark, but after a few moments, her eyes adjusted. Waterbearers thrive in darkness. Their blue eyes allow them to have excellent night vision.

"Who are you?" Chelan asked in a whisper.

"It doesn't matter who I am. I know you are innocent and want to help, but you must work with me."

"Why in the icy hell would I do that? Helping someone is what got me here."

"Because you will not have a fair opportunity to state your case if you don't work with me. Nahal doesn't want Elder Akay to hear your account. He would rather punish you in Tiber's place."

"Only a chief can decide that."

"Well, at the rate he's going, Nahal will be acting chief until the decree is found. It seems like you're okay with not getting a fair chance to account and would eagerly accept Tiber's punishment—"

"What do I need to do?"

"Tell the truth regardless of what happens. Only speak of what you know for certain. If you do this, you will be free. Once free, you will be in debt to me."

"In debt? Ugh, what would Tiber's punishment be?"

"Still wondering about that? If she's charged with murdering her father, she will face death. That means—"

"That I'll get lashes until she's found." Chelan groaned.

"Nahal thinks that you were negligent in letting her escape. He is furious over the chief's death, and he blames you. He would not mind leading people to think you were an accomplice."

"They can't do that to me. They must give me a chance to account. That's tribe law."

She remembered Nahal's vow: *At the end of the day, I want the best for our tribe. I'm willing to do whatever it takes for that to happen.*

"With Nahal as acting chief, it's in his hands, and he already has a following. If you want to gamble with your life, I'm leaving." Sita stood up.

"Wait! I'd bleed to death after a few days of consistent lashes. I'll do what you say. You have my word," Chelan whispered.

"Good, I'll make sure you get a fair chance to account." Sita hurriedly left the Cave of Shame. She went to her tent and changed back into her clothes. Running as fast as she could, she went to the medicine lair and made an energy tea. Pressed for time, she gave the guard some tea.

After several minutes, he started to stir, "Ugh, what! What happened?"

"Shh, I found you like this. You must be so tired, and I'm trying to get the rest of the tribesmen back in commission. Here, this tea will give you energy."

The guard hurried to his feet. "The tribe would kill me if Chelan escaped." He looked into the cave and sighed, "That was too close for comfort."

"Don't worry, I won't tell anyone," Sita promised.

The guard continued to drink the tea, "Thank you, Sita."

"Of course, it is my job to look after the well-being of this tribe, and I take that duty very seriously. You can return the cup to the medicine lair when you have time. Take care now." Sita walked away, looking back to wave at the guard.

She looked in the direction of Nahal's tent. It was dark. He must be sleeping. The idea of him gave her the chills.

She didn't understand why. Sita sighed. It was almost scary how things had been turning in such drastic directions for this tribe. She hoped that Tiber was okay. Needing to clear her head, she proceeded to her lair to check on the other tribesmen.

She headed straight to her spice corner and began mixing herbal leaves. Staying busy was the only way she could remain calm. A part of her was afraid she was making promises she could not keep. Protecting Tiber from the Cave of Shame was different from helping her overcome a murder investigation by their tribe. Now she has promised to help Chelan in exchange for his loyalty. She ground the leaves to a powder and continued to sort and organize. Sita sighed and instinctively looked at the moon. It was beautiful and calming. However, her tribe was known not to believe in the Universe. She wasn't sure if she genuinely believed in that or not. She was raised not to believe, but since her father passed on a hunting mission two years ago, she felt the moon almost calling out to her. In the time that passed since his death, she had become a woman and felt lost without him. The moon's presence felt comforting for Sita. It replicated the feeling of being able to run to her father for protection. Gazing at the luminous sphere, Sita felt confident, fearless, and determined.

Whether or not she had been raised as a believer, she was raised to know right from wrong. Neither Nahal nor Tiber were willing to state the entire situation. Nahal had questionable tactics, but so did Tiber. Only a fair chance to account with Elder Akay would determine where she stood. She knew in her heart that neither of them were bad people. Sita knew she had to fight for that, ensuring her tribe's brothers and sisters received equality. And she would not stop until they obtained it.

After making herbal powders, she cleaned the tribesmen's wounds again. Of the twenty men that were brought to her, five of them had passed shortly after she began tending to them. She noticed that a sword had slashed them all. That was not a typical Waterbearer tribe weapon. They preferred to use spears, bows, and arrows in the Tribe of Snow and Ice and the Jungle Tribe. The Beach tribe mainly used spears and tridents. The Windmasters predominantly used their signature wind blade. In some cases, they also used various daggers—frequently a push dagger. The Landkeepers didn't use weapons often. They are physically the strongest people on the planet, with Firehearts coming in a close second.

However, the Windmasters proved that outstanding strategy and clever maneuvering could trump physical strength. Landkeepers' primary weapon choice was a scythe or battle axe if a weapon was to be used at all. Now, the Firehearts did use swords a lot. But in complete fairness, their people were the most well-versed in all sorts of weaponry, including morning stars, throwing knives, archery, and battle axes. Sita knew every nation had exceptions and didn't press the issue further. She just hoped that whoever did this would not catch up to Tiber.

After checking on the tribesmen and redressing necessary wounds, she returned to her tent. She knew exactly how she would get Chelan an opportunity with Elder Akay. She just needed perfect timing. She untied her dark brown curly hair from its sloppy bun, letting it go free, and made twists before going to bed. With fragments of night remaining, she closed her eyes, hoping that Tiber would be all right.

CHAPTER 5

When morning came, Sita rose early. After washing up and getting ready for the day, she checked on the tribesmen. Two of them were conscious. However, they didn't seem to remember what had happened to them. Sita was discouraged. If they had remembered something, it could have helped Tiber. She saw Nahal leave his father's tent and proceed to the elder's tent.

Why are my eyes always finding him?

"Sita, is there anything I can help with?" Shasa came into the lair.

"Oh, not at all. You really need to be taking it easy." Sita pretended to be busy until she saw Shasa from the corner of her eye. "Shasa, what's wrong? Have you been crying?" Sita stopped everything and hurried to her tribe sister's side.

Shasa was wiping tears from her eyes. "They all think that Tiber killed our father. And worse, the tribesmen went on an early patrol and didn't find her. I feel so horrible. I wish my father were here," Shasa sobbed.

"Shh, Shasa, this isn't good for you and the baby. I personally do not believe that Tiber would kill anyone. I think that something was bothering her, though. Maybe she went to the chief about it. I hate to say this, but she may have found him dead and tried to help him when Nahal walked in. If he found Tiber bloody, it would be a bit suspicious that, as the chief's daughter, she didn't call for help. But we won't know unless we can find her and she gets the chance to account before Elder Akay. She has the gift of Moonsense. Only she would know if Tiber was telling the truth."

"Speaking of truth, I can't believe she would lie at the first meeting. I'm just so confused. What doesn't she trust us with? What doesn't she trust me with?" Shasa started crying again. Sita hugged her, trying to soothe her. She saw Nahal leave the elder's tent. When he looked in her direction, Sita looked away, hoping he hadn't caught her staring at him.

"It seems like Nahal is doing his best to keep the tribe together," Sita whispered to Shasa.

"Seems like he is trying to push his opinion about my sister onto the tribe." She shook her head slowly. "What am I saying? He's just trying to help, and he's been working hard at keeping peace and order in the tribe. Honestly, it's been comforting seeing him lead the young men in stepping up for the tribe. He may have a chance at standing in as chief until my father's decree is found. It's so odd that it's missing," Shasa sighed.

"It's missing? That is odd. We are having a meeting about Chelan soon. You should try and rest. I'll check on you later if I have some spare time." Sita and Shasa embraced, and the latter left the lair. After ensuring that Shasa was gone, Sita hurried to the elder's tent.

The meeting was starting in the Cave of Shame. Chelan was hog-tied in the prison crate. Yelling and shouting proceeded as Nahal walked in. All eyes were on him. He felt the pulse of the tribe and wanted swift justice for Chief Dalit. However, he noticed some of the tribe seemed to disapprove of their lead warrior being hog-tied and humiliated. Nahal raised his hand, and everyone went quiet.

"Everyone, thank you for your cooperation. As we know, Tiber murdered her father, but she was supposed to be guarded in the medicine lair by Chelan, the lead warrior. However, he abandoned his post, allowing her to escape. His negligence must be punished. Do you have anything to say for yourself, Chelan?"

Chelan strained his neck, "I was not negligent! Sita passed out from exhaustion, and I took her to her tent to try and help her. Tiber was still unconscious when I left. I did not leave my post. My duty was to guard the medicine lair. To guard means to protect and defend. I did protect and defend as I knew how."

"But you left Tiber to sneak out and kill her father. On the slim chance that she didn't kill him, you allowed the opportunity for him to be killed. His death is your fault, regardless of how you look at it. So, your blabbing about protecting and defending is a bunch of lies," Nahal retorted.

"Hold on now, son." Elder Akay shuffled into the cave, supported by Sita. "Chelan was honest in his account so far, and you should not be so quick to cast judgment and name him a liar. Chelan, son, did you know that Tiber was awake?"

"No, ma'am."

"Were you concerned when Sita passed out?"

"I was deeply worried for her health."

Nahal took a slight step back at hearing Chelan's answer, causing Sita's face to flush.

"When you took Sita to her tent, do you know where Tiber went?"

"No, I do not."

Nahal rolled his eyes. "Elder Akay—"

"Tribe, Chelan answered honestly. He should not be subjected to this treatment since he proves to be an honest brother," Elder Akay spoke.

"My beloved Elder," cerulean-eyed Mahak said, "although I agree with you completely that Chelan was not involved in the murder of our chief. We should consider a mild punishment because he left his post's physical location. If this had not occurred, our chief may still be alive. And if death was inevitable, we would have been positioned to catch the murderer."

"You are right, and that is in accord with our laws. But you men can decide that. Sita, I want to keep stretching my legs. Come help me." Elder Akay continued walking through the Cave of Shame with Sita's assistance.

"Tribe, I have been corrected by the elders. Chelan's punishment will not be based on Chief Dalit's murder. He will be removed from guard duty for a month and removed from the position of lead warrior, per our laws," Nahal concluded. The tribe cheered for Nahal as he untied Chelan. The cheering and clapping were so loud that no one could hear Nahal's words to Chelan, "I apologize for this. I feared you were in on the murder plot and had a lapse of judgment. Forgive me, brother."

"It is in the past now. I accept your apology. I will commit to being more diligent on whatever post entrusted to me from now on." Chelan nodded and exited the Cave of Shame. Nahal dismissed the tribe and proceeded to follow the direction Sita and Elder Akay went. The pair had not gone too far.

"Elder Akay," Nahal hurried to catch up, "thank you for your words. They were a great help in achieving justice and equality. Thank you, ma'am. Sita, may I have a moment?"

"Um, I was help—"

"Child, I can manage. Go and enjoy some time with Nahal before he gets too popular with the ladies."

Sita cleared her throat before Nahal grabbed her hands, gently pulling her toward the cave entrance. Her pulse began racing at the coolness of his hands on hers.

"Did you want to talk about something, Nahal?"

"Yeah, I want to check on you. I wish you had told me that you passed out. You have been working so hard. The tribe needs you, so you must take care of yourself. You can come and talk to me whenever you need anything, okay?"

Their faces were so close that the misty clouds that formed from their breath immediately became one as they exhaled.

"Thank you." A sweet silence consumed the atmosphere, and Sita struggled to pull her gaze away from him.

"I have some things to attend to in the lair. Don't be a stranger." Sita smiled at Nahal and gently pulled away from him.

"I won't be. Remember what I said, I'll do whatever it takes to protect this tribe."

"So will I," she replied.

Nahal smirked and winked at her before she left to go to the medicine lair. She paced herself as she approached the lair, not wanting Nahal to think she was running from him. Once she arrived, she was happy to see that another group of tribesmen was awake. She prepared them for a final examination before returning them to their regular duties. She sighed out of frustration. Once again, none of them could remember anything about what happened the day of the attack. Sita almost wanted to knock her head against the wall when the tall, broad-shouldered Chelan entered.

"I'm here to start repaying my debt," his deep, booming voice called out.

"Shut up, will you! Coming in here shouting like that," Sita yelled.

"Sorry, but who's yelling now," Chelan whispered, playfulness twinkling in his midnight blue eyes.

Sita asked him, "How did you know it was me?"

"Just because I got knocked out doesn't make me stupid. I thought it was you when you started talking. When you returned to bring the guard that tea, it confirmed it for me. Thanks, I appreciate it." He squeezed her in a tight, suffocating hug.

"Let go! Okay, listen, meet me at the river after dinner. We're going hunting." Sita smiled.

"Okay, I still don't know what's going on, but I'll be there." Chelan raised his thick, long, dark-brown eyebrows before turning on his heels to leave.

CHAPTER 6

Tiber's dark blue eyes fluttered open. The pain had subsided. She struggled to sit up, but when she looked down, her mouth dropped open in disbelief. She had just survived the Changing. She was officially a woman. Her body looked completely different. The changes that took years for the average pubescent girl happened overnight, as it is for every Snow tribe girl.

Tiber cried a little. If only her father had lived another day, he would have seen her fully become a woman. The sadness in her only deepened when she looked around for Mika. She must be okay—she left on her own. But her absence only brought the harsh reality that Tiber was all alone. She turned over and struggled to stand up, her body still aching from the Changing. The newfound tightness of her clothes made any movement unwelcome. Tiber knew she was in the Jungle tribe, but she was still close to the border. She had to move deeper into the lush jungle to have a chance to survive her tribe's wrath. With every step she took, Tiber yearned for Mika's quiet company. She came upon a stream cleverly hidden by the thick of the forest roots. Quickly, she made for it, only to be knocked backward by a panther.

Once the cat looked at her, it released her and continued to the stream. Those eyes were unmistakable. "Mika?"

The panther stopped and turned toward Tiber. She reached out her hand to touch the flank where Mika had been injured. The panther growled.

"Mika, it's me, Tiber. Mika? Don't you remember?"

The panther leaped and licked Tiber's face. It was Mika. She never knew that her pet would experience the Changing too. Tiber remembered that her father wanted her to keep Mika. Did he know that this would happen?

She pushed those thoughts aside as she was parched and hungry. When she looked at her reflection, she was taken aback. She knew that her body had changed, but her face was fuller, and her eyes were more piercing against her chestnut complexion. Tiber stood up. The seams near her chest and hips were stressed and, in some places, ripped by her new shape. She looked like a different person. No wonder Mika hadn't recognized her.

Mika drank sloppily from the stream. Tiber looked up; it was midday. She smiled and quickly returned to where they had tried to recover. She grabbed her bag and small belongings and hurried back to Mika.

"Look at us, girl. No one would ever recognize us. What are the chances of this happening?" She retrieved a small hunting dagger from her bag and pulled her hair into a bun. In one smooth motion, she cut the bun off her head and caught it before it touched the water. When she looked at her reflection again, her long locks of dark brown hair were now a short inverted bob.

"New look for me, new look for you, and now I just need a new name." She thought for a moment. "Talia, I will tell them my name is Talia. Let's go, Mika. We have a lot to do." She slowly mounted the cat. Tiber was thankful that Mika was strong enough to handle her weight, but she wasn't going to push Mika to run. She decided they needed to go to the Jungle tribe where she could sell her hair for a price and possibly find an ally.

Tiber was a little worried about the Jungle tribe. They were staunch believers in the Universal Order. However, with everything that had transpired, she was left with no other choice. She couldn't risk being caught by the World Order, which would mean a death sentence. She failed a critical mission, and with Nahal against her, she could never go back, not until her name was cleared. Despite this, the moon showed her kindness and mercy. Maybe Aqila wasn't so crazy after all. She wasn't entirely sure that she was right, but Tiber had nothing else to go with.

After two hours of traveling, Tiber and Mika stopped for a rest. She felt a little relieved. Her tribe would never come looking for her here. If anything, they would alert Chiefess Marina and the Beach tribe. But the Snow tribe and the Jungle tribe were not on good terms. Tiber's attention was captured by a juicy piece of fruit hanging from a tall tree with a thick trunk. She was famished. After kicking off her boots, the Changing didn't make her much taller, she struggled to make the climb. She stretched as far as she could to reach the fruit. It was almost within reach, but before her fingers could grab it, a selfish little monkey snatched it up. Tiber groaned and went to swat at the monkey. The animal responded by showing Tiber its teeth.

Icy hell! Sharp teeth!

This startled her, and she lost her grip on the trunk, banging her head on the jungle floor.

She opened her eyes, her head spinning a bit. When she sat up, three spearheads were deathly close to her face.

"Who are you?" a rather large man asked her. His face, hands, and arms were painted with turquoise, so much so that Tiber couldn't tell what his complexion was. When she looked around, everyone had paint on their body.

A woman's voice called out, "Answer or the panther dies!"

"No, Mika! Stop, please. I'm lost. I was just trying to eat. Please stop." Tiber fought back the tears. The woman was the owner of a ferocious jaguar, whose massive paws were on Mika's neck, pinning her down. "Stop, my cat is hurt!" Her eyes found the river, and then her soul claimed it. As the painted people approached closer, Tiber pushed them all back with a massive wave of water. One of the men was knocked unconscious as his head connected with the tree's trunk. She created a protective ring of water around her and Mika, seeing that the jaguar was pushed aside. One man and the woman remained, also using the river to fight Tiber back.

As the battle became more heated, Tiber turned the river into ice. Her attackers could not continue to use it as a source once it was iced over. She then cocooned the last man into an ice cube. Now it was a one-on-one battle. The girl was a fierce opponent. Her combat skills were on par. Tiber could not fight like her, especially not barefoot, so she relied heavily on the use of water. The ground was drenched as a violent fight continued between the two. She called on her jaguar. Mika tried to protect Tiber from the jaguar, but the wild jungle cat was too strong. Tiber turned the wet jungle floor into a sheet of ice, causing the woman to slip, clutching her ankle. The jaguar hurried beside its master before Tiber found herself tied by vines to the point she could not escape. A vine wrapped around her throat; she dared not move. The feeling of suffocation reminded her of Aqila's raging to the point Tiber was instantly paralyzed.

"What is going on here?" a man with teal blue eyes asked.

"This girl is an intruder," the woman stated.

"Kano and Rio, bring the girl back. Rilian, tend to them," he said, pointing to the other two men, "then return to the tribe."

The girl named Rilian bowed her head, "Yes, Cove."

The men covered in paint drug Tiber and Mika, entangled in vines, through the jungle. Tiber wasn't sure what would happen next, but she reassured herself with the thought that if they had wanted her dead, they would have killed her already. Unable to summon any water due to the lack of circulation in her hands from the tightness of the vines, she was trapped. She hoped that things would not get any worse.

CHAPTER 7

Deep in the forest of Lower Ember, it was late afternoon. Arrow stood on the border of Ember and Pyroc, gazing lovingly toward his homeland. He gently touched the ring necklace Calida had given him. His mind swirled with thoughts of her—her laugh, her smile, the sound of her voice ringing throughout the room. He missed every bit of her. His eyes watered a bit. His soul was still torn. It was hard to lead the Flamethrowers, but it was even harder living in a world without Calida.

"Arrow?"

He shook himself free from his thoughts, "Yes, Yuuna?"

"Jai is back. The mission was successful," Yuuna spoke gently.

"Are the others back?"

"Not yet. However, I have the most updated report ready whenever you have time to look at it."

"Any word from Cahya?"

"No, we still haven't heard anything from him. Now that Jai's back, you want me to send the messenger hawk to Aqila?"

"Yes, you can send the message. Also, update the rest of the Flamethrowers after I meet with Jai and Aqila."

"Are you sure that you don't want to update them . . ."

"Could you, please."

"Are you doing all right?"

"You're asking because?"

"Because," she paused before turning his head to face her, "if you're not okay, you won't tell anyone."

Arrow allowed himself to relax upon meeting her gaze. "I'm getting better. Everything is still raw, but having this support system helps. I appreciate your concern." He patted her shoulder. The familiarity of having another Pyrocean was comforting to Arrow.

The pair hurried to the new headquarters, where they went their separate ways. He saw Jai waiting for him near the cabin door.

"It's good to see you again, Arrow. How . . . how are you doing?"

"I'm doing fine, Jai. Thanks for asking. Now, how did things go with Arin and Alena?"

"Everything went well—at least according to plan. Alena and Arin were able to pin his frequent locations. Tonight, Alena should be able to make contact, so I should hear from Arin by tomorrow morning," Jai explained.

"That's good, and I hope everything goes well. How are you handling your ability?"

"It's getting harder to control now that I'm getting stronger, but I'm managing to keep up."

"Glad to hear it. I'm waiting to hear from Aqila within the next day. I heard she's been swamped now that she's a Seer and stuff."

Jai almost jumped at the word "Seer" knowing Aqila's true identity. "Yeah, I bet she's . . . busy."

"What's up?" Arrow questioned.

"Nothing, I'm just a little tired, that's all."

"That's understandable. Just make yourself at home."

"Hey, have you heard from Cahya?"

"No, nothing," Arrow huffed.

"Well, it has only been two weeks. Give him time. He'll come back around."

"I don't know. I wonder if he's upset that Calida asked me to succeed her. I didn't expect her to ask that of me."

"No one expected Agni to be that strong. And we definitely didn't expect to lose anyone. All you can do is honor her request as best as you can."

Arrow sighed, "I will do my best. Jai, have you ever made a promise that you can't keep?"

"I have. I promised someone that I'd always be there for them and I wasn't. I also promised someone that I'd never forget them. . . and I did."

"It's an awful feeling. I almost hate myself for it."

"I understand, it's a terrible feeling. What happened?"

"This stays between us, please. I—I don't think I can keep my promise to Calida. I don't know what I was thinking! I can't lead the Flamethrowers—not forever. I mean, I never thought I'd ever go back to Pyroc, much less make amends with my family. I love being a Flamethrower. Really, I do. But, my dragon energy, it's never been so alive. Jai, I'm a Pyrocean. Eventually, I must go home; I must be among other dragons. I guess I was so overwhelmed by Calida's death that I promised her I'd lead them. I wanted her to die as peacefully as possible. Now, I feel guilty. I miss her every day. I loved her. I know I did. So why can't I hold the torch she passed to me? Why?"

"Arrow, you're being too hard on yourself. You're a Pyrocean and a royal; you can't change that. You tried to reinvent yourself to cope with your exile. Now that season is over, and that person you tried to become is slipping away because it was never you to begin with. You can't help who you are. Arrow, it was you who made me realize that in my own life. I can't help that I'm a Legend. I can try to run from that fate, but I will never escape it. You do miss Calida, and you did love her. You admired her. And Calida was an incredible young woman. She will always have a special place in your heart. But you're a Pyrcoean royal with a powerful dragon. She would have wanted you to embrace that, and she'd understand."

Tears slipped down Arrow's face, "Thanks."

"Do your best leading them for now, and when it feels right, pass the torch to someone else."

Arrow wiped his eyes, "Do you think Zay will join us?"

Realizing that Arrow was changing the topic, Jai replied, "I can't say for sure, but since he's defied Agni, he has no money and nowhere in Lower Ember to go. He can't live in Upper Ember without money. I can't say he'll like it here, but he would be an incredible asset to the team. The real question is, will he be accepted? He doesn't have an ability. I'm not sure how he will adapt to being a Flamethrower."

"I will accommodate him as much as he allows me. I'm going hunting for a bit." Arrow went to leave, and Yuuna met him at the door.

"Arrow, I have already hunted. We have enough food. I have also restocked the reserve, so we have plenty of dried food." Yuuna stopped him, placing her hand gently on his chest.

"Yeah, thanks. I just need a little fresh air. I'll be back." He brushed past her and continued to leave.

Yuuna sighed as she followed Arrow, leaving Jai standing alone.

Much had happened in the past two weeks. Zay fled Tora's house shortly after he recovered. Alena went after him and has been staying on his trail. Cahya hadn't reached out to anyone since Calida's death.

Arrow had expressed interest in making Cahya his second-in-command. However, until he returns, Yuuna has been diligently working in his place. Arrow believed that Cahya would be eager to return if the leadership of the Flamethrowers were in his hands.

Aqila went back home for the time being. She said Kavi agreed to see what he could learn regarding Agni's and Neptune's claims to power. After Zay left, Aqila suggested making him a part of the Flamethrowers, an offer that would benefit both sides. Zay would have a home and the necessities of living, and the Flamethrowers would gain valuable insight into Agni's inner workings. Sheraga went home, saying that he had urgent matters to tend to.

The rest of the Flamethrowers were scattered about with their duties for the rebuilding phase. Arrow and Suvan quickly rebuilt the new headquarters, which was about three miles from the old cabin. It had the same layout as the cabin. Jai headed to the back to unroll his blanket and rest. As he lay down, he thought about how much his powers had grown. A month ago, he could barely hold a flame. Now light and fire were second nature to him. The life source running through his veins was the passion for his Element and the drive to be a better Legend than his predecessor.

Late evening was quickly turning into night. He hoped that Arin and Alena were doing okay. He wasn't sure if anyone could be successful in converting Zay into a Flamethrower, but it wouldn't hurt to try. Jai was hopeful that he could reform himself into a better person. There was another thing plaguing his mind: the other two Legends.

Who could they be? If I am the sign of the rebirth of the four, who are the other two? There should be one from the Waterbearer tribes and one from the Landkeepers. What if the Waterbearer is a supporter of Neptune and his vision for the Worldly Order? What if the Landkeeper is involved in Theyra's civil war? Is it possible for Aqila and I to right the wrongs of our predecessors without the other half of the Legends present? Sometimes it takes years for all four Legends to meet. Would we meet the same fate? Can the world wait that long?

The squawk of a messenger hawk pulled Jai away from these frantic thoughts. As he approached the door, he realized that he was utterly alone. After retrieving the message, he sent the bird off. His heart began beating faster when he read the two words scribbled on the tiny piece of paper, "Move in." This was his cue—time to go back to the heart of Lower Ember, it was time to go home.

CHAPTER 8

The sun had set about an hour ago, and the stars performed an elaborate dance in the skies above. Alena's light brown eyes twinkled against the glimmering of the moon. Her gaze was focused on her target. She covered her body in a plain black cloak. This part of Lower Ember was like an ancient village. Her target was rummaging behind a market stand. Very few people were walking about. Those who went by didn't care that someone's goods were stolen right before their eyes.

The target would look up every so often, hopeful of getting enough before the owner came. It would not be wise to approach him now, so she waited. Five minutes passed, and her target had every pocket on his body filled with food. Pushing all emotions aside, she followed several yards behind. The target's destination was a modest little home. As he went inside, she saw the modest light of a candle flicker. The closer she came, she noticed that the door was not completely closed. Alena found this unusual. Nonetheless, this did not stop her from pushing the door further open very slowly. Once open, she saw him sitting at a small round table with a slight smile.

"Close the door behind you," he smirked.

Alena's breath got caught in her throat as she wondered how he came to expect her. She slowly shut the door behind her.

"Make yourself at home."

"How?"

"How what? How did I know you were following me? You've been following me for weeks. I must say, you're not too great at your job. Pretty sloppy, actually."

Alena rushed toward him with a fist of flames, which he caught easily. He twisted her wrist slightly, causing the fire to cease. She was uncomfortable in his grip but not in any pain. If he wanted to hurt her, he would have.

"Are we doing this again? You can't beat me at my own game. Now, if you want to talk, let's sit down and be civil . . . for as long as we can."

Zay let her wrist go and sat down before motioning for Alena to sit across from him. She looked around apprehensively as she slowly sat at the table.

"What do you want? You're not here to say hello." He grabbed an apple from his pocket and began eating it.

"How could you just leave like that? How can you walk around like nothing happened?"

"Why would I stay? I think that's the better question to ask. For everyone to question me—for your allies to doubt me when I said that I turned on Agni—to be asked who Agni is and where he goes, only for them to be dissatisfied when I say that I don't know. Tell me, what did I have to gain by staying?"

"Zay, we want to give you a chance," Alena started.

"Really? Then why were you tailing me like the target in the center of a bull's eye for two weeks? How come today is the first day you approached me? You've been watching me from a distance with your little twin like I'm prey, and I'm just supposed to trust you because you asked?"

"I stayed in that house waiting for you to wake up and talk to me. I wanted everyone to see you for who you really are. But before you gave me a chance, you just left."

"Why are you making this so personal? You don't know me!"

"Because you saved my life, Zay, twice. And you have no idea how it felt to watch you bleed out, taking a blow that was meant for me. You have no idea how it felt as the building collapsed, knowing that you might have died before I had a chance even to say thank you. I don't know you, but I know you aren't a bad person."

"I—I know somewhere, I'm not a bad person. I've done some things I'm not proud of, but I did it to survive."

"I'm here for you, Zay; give me a chance to prove it."

Zay's eyes locked on Alena's for a long time. He sighed, "All right, Alena, what do you want to talk about?"

"Come and join the Flamethrowers—"

"Hot as hell, no! Why would I do that?"

"So you can have a better life!"

"How? Maybe you didn't notice. I can't throw flames, and I don't have an Element like the rest of you."

"Why are you saying that like it's a limitation? You have fought against several of us and won because you're a great fighter, Zay. You don't have any other friends. You're dancing in the shadows to avoid showing your face in this trodden village. You steal just to get by. You don't have a permanent place to stay. Why not?"

"I can't deal with Jai right now. I just can't," Zay groaned.

"Why?"

"If I tell you this, you can't ever tell anyone. I'm taking a chance to trust you with a secret, like you took this chance to drop your guard and confront me, knowing that I can beat you in a fight." He chuckled. He offered her an apple, which she received and began to eat. Zay began sharing his secret with Alena. She listened to every word that fell from his lips, feeling his pains and emotions. His bottled-up feelings and anger fueled his rage and misguided him. The more he spoke, the more she could tell he was freeing himself from what haunted him.

*****

"Arin," Jai called softly.

"Jai, I'm so glad you're here. Alena's message said to meet her here, but she never came this way. There were no signs of her. I was worried about going back. The last time I contacted her was two days ago."

"Does she have a reason to shake you off the trail?"

"No, why would she?"

"I'm just asking, Arin. Well, I think she wouldn't be too far off. This is where Zay normally resides."

"In this beat-down place?"

"Yeah, he had a hard childhood."

"I can't imagine even being able to enjoy a childhood here."

The town was desolate. There was a wooden cart in the street filled with rotting fruit. The pungent smell permeated the entire area. There was no grass—only loose dirt covering the ground. The tiny wooden structures were sorry attempts at housing with their falling planks and caved-in roofs. The dirt paths were lined with people in tattered blankets, shivering outside in the brisk wind. Women cradled their thin, bony children close to their breasts in a futile attempt to keep them warm on this cool night. These were the Giftless.

"I know. Most of Lower Ember is no different than here. However, this part of town is the most run-down. I lived not too far from here. It was a little better than this place. Zay and I weren't friends growing up. He wasn't a bad person. He just had a lot of rough situations. His mother went blind when he was eight or so. He stopped going to the town school to take care of her. Work was hard to come by for an eight-year-old, so he pretty much stole in the market to have food to eat. He got in a lot of fights, and trust me, he wasn't above slashing your ears and nearly cutting your eyes out. But he did his best to ensure his mother was okay. And she loved him so much. She died when he was fifteen. Without her constant love, he was subject to the harsh reality of the miserable place called Lower Ember."

"What makes you believe in him like you do?"

"I know he's a good person because I've seen him do much good. If he stole some fruit, he would give it all to kids who were homeless and go hungry himself for the day. He gave his outgrown clothes to kids in need. He'd do random favors for the elderly, and if they gave him two coins, he'd take one and give one. And he was always honest in his intentions. And the truth is, if I didn't have Arka, I'm not sure I could have been half the man he turned out to be."

Arin gently touched his shoulder. "This is all the more reason he deserves a fresh start."

Jai sighed, "That's my and Aqila's thoughts exactly." Arin began to fidget when he brought her name up. "I'm going to stop talking about her if it makes you uncomfortable."

"No! I'm fine! I—it's just different. I mean, you're fire, and she's wind. I don't know . . ." Arin swallowed.

"Yes, my friend, and our ally. She's done a lot to help our cause. I feel you're not comfortable talking to me about your distrust for her."

"It's not distrust! She has shown that she's truly an advocate for our cause. I—I just feel like she's doing more for you than I— than we are," she explained.

"How so? I'd still be stuck in a village just like this if I hadn't met Arrow."

"I just see how both of you relate on a different level," Arin started.

Then there was a sudden sound of footsteps. Jai and Arin readied themselves.

"Hey, the mission was successful. Zay agreed to at least meet with Arrow and discuss possibly joining us. He's packing some of his things, so I'll wait for him here." Alena emerged from the shadows.

"What's that smell?"

"Oh, I just ate an apple," Alena answered.

"You ate there! What if it was poison?"

Jai shook his head. "Arin, simmer down." He rubbed her shoulders up and down as if she had been cold.

"Sh—Shouldn't Jai take him to Arrow?" Arin stuttered.

"He doesn't trust anyone. That's why I led you to another part of town. Sorry, Arin, I wanted to ensure we ended the mission successfully. We had gone two weeks with no luck. I just had to try it my way."

Arin was surprised. "No, no, okay. I understand. We'll just head back; be careful and send a signal if anything goes awry."

Jai touched Arin's shoulder. "If Alena put this much thought into things and has earned Zay's trust, I think everything will be fine. Alena, just be back by the hour." Jai pulled Arin by the hand and headed back toward the new headquarters.

Jai could sense Arin's heightened frustration, which painfully bothered him. She was fuming inside, yet desperately trying to keep calm.

"You'll feel better once you let it out," he whispered.

"Ugh, why did she think it was better to go alone like that? What if something happened, and I had to tell Arrow? She didn't think about that, now did she? I don't understand why she gets so defensive about Zay. I know he saved her life and all, but still."

Jai began to laugh. "I guess she cares. Seeing Agni stab Zay from his back through his stomach was scary. He tried to protect her and nearly paid with his life. Everyone expresses their care a little differently."

"I care about all of the Flamethrowers, and I worry about not doing enough for them and not being what they need."

"Wow, you finally said it!"

"Don't laugh at me." Arin playfully bumped his shoulder.

"No, don't take it the wrong way. I'm honestly relieved that you trusted me with your feelings. I notice how hard you try to be there for everyone, and I appreciate how you've been there for me. This would be a lot harder without your support."

Whoa, what am I saying?

"Thanks, Jai." She smiled as they headed back to their new cabin. "So, will you be meeting with Zay when he comes to the cabin?"

"Probably not. If Arrow wants me to, yeah, but I don't want to muddle the roles within the Flamethrowers. Especially since he has not named a second-in-command." Jai paused. "I don't know why he hasn't chosen Yuuna yet. She has been really on top of things. Arrow hasn't been himself since Calida, and we understand that, which makes Yuuna's job much harder. She's giving Arrow and the Flamethrowers her all."

"I think Arrow is waiting for Cahya to return and name him second-in-command. Cahya is a master of his Element and has learned many advanced forms. His people skills need work, though."

"Yeah, which is why Yuuna would be great."

"Not happening. Arrow recruited her because she wasn't making the cut in the DragonLord's army. She came from a military Pyrocean family and was discharged due to failing status in her prerequisites, which would have been a disgrace to her family. When she first arrived, she was over the stars for Arrow, but we all know how that panned out."

"And that's not a sound reason to withhold an opportunity to excel. The only thing that should matter is that she's doing a good job."

The pair made it back to the cabin. Upon entering, Yuuna's pretty face and amber eyes appeared. "Jai and Arin, is the status of said operation successful?"

"Yes, Yuuna, report to Arrow that Alena and said target will be back within the hour," Arin replied.

"I made a note of it, thank you." She immediately turned her attention to other matters.

"Let's get something to eat while we wait for Alena and Zay," Jai suggested to Arin.

"Sure, look, Suvan and Dysis are over there with what looks like a couple of recruits," Arin noticed. The pair went to the center of the room, awaiting their turn to introduce themselves.

CHAPTER 9

Aqila hurried out of the Capitol. She sighed into the night with the yellow stone of her hairpin flitting about in the starlight.

"Well, it seems like you met the same dismay I faced earlier," Kavi's voice called out to her as he waited.

"I didn't think our families would be so disappointed about moving the wedding date out. You know, most families, statistically speaking, are concerned about their youth advancing too quickly in these matters. Our parents are worried we are moving too slowly."

"You didn't see it coming? After pushing the wedding out by ten months? I did! My mother loves weddings. I think she was planning my wedding day the moment I was born," Kavi chuckled.

"I know. It's just that this really isn't a good time. I mean, there's Jai, Agni, and now Neptune. Currently, Kashmala and Wyndhm aren't involved, but I fear we could get pulled in if we keep letting this linger."

"You don't have to explain yourself to me. I understand, but I fear our parents are worried that we are getting cold feet, although we know we are not. It may be necessary that we arrange an event to showcase a little public display of affection. I think that would put our families at ease."

"What do you have in mind?"

"Why don't we organize an engagement gala? We could plan some festivities open to both Kashmala and Wyndhm. Also, it would allow our families to see how well we work together on a grand scale." Kavi held Aqila's hand, intertwining his fingers with hers.

"You are always the man with a plan that always works. Set a date, and we can go from there." Aqila lovingly glanced at Kavi. She grazed his jawline with her fingertips. Kavi closed his eyes at her touch. Smiling, she looked up to the stars, and a tingling sensation began to wash over her. She saw Cahya in Upper Ember with an arrow on fire, followed by multiple arrows on fire. Then she saw Arrow and Jai in Lower Ember. Lastly, there was a gold mask floating in the water.

Aqila slowly shook her head. "I'm glad you're back." Kavi chuckled.

"Kavi, I—"

"I know, just tell me where you have to go and when."

"Upper Ember—something's up with Cahya. I don't need to leave immediately, though. So, I'll plan to leave within a few days. I promise to write down my half of the festivities for the engagement gala and personally deliver it to you before I go."

"I love the sound of that, my love. Be safe, and let me know if you need me for anything. And I mean anything!"

"I know, and I will. Also, for the record, I can't wait to spend some quality time together during our engagement gala." She brushed her nose to his before parting ways.

"I share the sentiment; it's quite overdue. Aqila, what colors do you want for the engagement gala?"

"What colors do you have in mind?"

"Well, every rulership wedding must be silver and white. So let's get creative with this one," Kavi suggested.

"Your favorite color is blue and mine is yellow. How about a turquoise and yellow theme?"

"Sounds good to me. Well, good night. I will see you in the morning," Kavi said as he reentered the Capitol. Aqila sighed as she watched his broad back and long locks of gray hair disappear. She continued toward the mountain edge, where Talon was faithfully waiting.

"It's quite late for you to be out, Aqila. Is everything going all right with the wedding plans?" Saar playfully nudged her arm as she mounted her dasher.

"Let's just say it's coming," she sighed.

"What's wrong, Storm? This is the day you've been waiting for," Saar gently spoke.

"It's nothing like that. We just wanted to push the wedding out, and our mothers almost passed out over the thought of it. Your father says Kavi's wedding is his top priority, so pushing the date out is not ideal. The only one in our corner was my father."

"Wait, Kavi is all right with this?"

"Well, I expressed that I'm still involved with Jai's situation and getting visions concerning him. I can't just drop it like nothing has happened. Saar, when we get married, I want us to have some time together, not interrupted by urgent world affairs."

"Well, you've got the right man then. That's my brother. If I were getting married, I wouldn't want to wait. I will be all in, starting my new chapter in life with my wife. Either way, you two are intelligent, so I'm supporting you every step of the way."

"Thanks, Saar. Have a good night." Aqila held her breath as she urged Talon to fly.

Is Kavi more disappointed than he let on? We have been waiting a long time for this. Maybe I'm asking too much of him. Let me not assume anything. If he weren't okay with it, he would tell me, wouldn't he?

They headed toward Zeroun's house in the mountains. Aqila decided to stay there until the wedding. She would get a couple of visitors looking for visions, so having the same location for a while was helpful to her people.

She settled Talon for the night and walked through the door, stepping over a pile of letters. Her mind began racing with thoughts of Cahya. She sat with her legs folded.

"All right, Cahya, what's going on?" Aqila muttered. "He hasn't reached out to Arrow, but there's an arrow on fire, and then it multiplies. Is he recruiting? But why if he still has a rift with Arrow? Maybe he's trying to show the Flamethrowers that he would have made a better leader. But it doesn't fit Cahya's personality. He's not a showoff. Regardless, he has something going on. Maybe Arrow is not doing a great job leading because of Calida's death, and Cahya is trying to take charge. But, if Arrow had just been bombing it, I would have gotten something from the Flamethrowers before now. All right, I do know that Cahya is building something. Since that's a fact, Jai needs to know and check it out and show support if he's doing a good thing." Aqila stood up, finally feeling some relief.

Whenever someone desired an insight, they could slide a letter under the front door. Since the house was secured using wind bolts, an intricate lock with hollow chambers that could only be unlocked by channeling the exact amount of wind to release the bolt, it was secure. Only a Windmaster could unlock the doors and windows of Zeroun's house. And not just any Windmaster, they had to be skilled enough to allocate the appropriate amount of wind to release the bolt.

She picked up the letters from the floor and began reviewing them.

"Arrow, Sheraga, Tora, and Boaz." There were multiple letters from Boaz. She had not talked to him in weeks. "Maybe he would want to accompany me when I visit Jai and Arrow. Hmm, that would also ease Kavi's mind a bit." Aqila sat at the marble stone table, and after setting up her quill and ink, she began to write replies. Then something flagged in her mind. She looked around, and multiple things were slightly off from where she had last remembered leaving them. She looked at the floor. There were skid marks from where the table and chairs had been moved. Aqila started for the kitchen drawers. Her long, slender fingers grazed her and Zeroun's letterbox. All of the important letters were kept there. However, the lid was slightly ajar. She would have never left it like that.

Someone's been here?

CHAPTER 10

The night was far from young. Tiber and Mika had been tied up for hours, sitting in a tent far away from the rest of the Jungle tribe. Fearing their chief would alert her tribe and send her back, she decided that she would rather die than face that fate. Struggling against the vines was no use. The man had a powerful mastery of his Element to hold such a grip even when he was not physically present.

The tent's flap moved, interrupting Tiber's thoughts, and the man who had entangled her walked in alone. He had a damp cloth in his hand. In one motion, he wiped the blue and green paint from the left side of his face and then the right side. His teal eyes were piercing yet gentle at the same. His skin was deep brown, and his short, wavy hair was several shades darker. He sat across the room, away from her. "So, just what are you doing venturing into my territory?" Although there was a slight air of hostility in his voice, Tiber found it unusually soothing.

"It's a long and miserable story," Tiber's voice shook.

"Well, how about this? I will release a vine every twenty minutes."

"The only thing I care about right now is not being sent back to my tribe."

"Do you fear for your life?"

Tiber nodded.

"Start talking," he demanded.

"I was working for Neptune, and a mission got really messed up. I captured the Windmaster Seer and made an honest mistake that almost killed her. My partner is also working for Neptune, and he betrayed me. He was fine with the Seer dying, and I wanted to save her. We fought, and the girl freed herself and fought us. She was a powerful Storm, and we were no match for her. She knocked us out. I woke up to find several of my tribesmen had been attacked too. My father, who is chief—was chief, held a council. I lied to everyone because I didn't want them to know I was working with Neptune. The crazy thing is that my partner lied too, but he mixed it with some truth. The whole problem fell on me, and I got locked up to await my punishment. I escaped to have an open and honest conversation with my father, but someone had attacked him before I got there. He gave me one last message before he died and told me to go. Then my partner walked in and blamed me for killing my father. The tribe believed him, and they shot my cat. We fell into the river, and we hid in the jungle."

"Why can't you go back and tell them the truth? You must have at least one Moonsayer for them to determine that you lied and your partner didn't. So go and tell the truth."

"We do, but they may kill me first because of my father's death, and I have no protection. The only thing I can do now is get the Seer to clear my name," Tiber was frantic.

All the vines that bound her were immediately released. "What? You believe me, just like that?"

"I could tell you were telling the truth," the man replied.

"That's impossible. Moonsayers are unique to my tribe." Tiber was shocked.

"Wrong. Moonsayers are gifted to Waterbearers only. Just like Seers are gifted to Windmasters only. Your tribe operates on many myths and superstitions. I believe they have allowed you to fall to the Worldly Order and in total opposition to the Universe. In the Jungle tribe, we are firm believers in the Universal Order. My name is Cove. I am a Moonsayer and the Chief of the Jungle Tribe. I will allow you to stay here and help you work out your delicate situation under several conditions.

Tiber groaned as she was untying Mika. "What conditions?"

"First, you must work hard like everyone else and pay for what you need. You're not staying for free. Second, I want all your leads on Neptune."

"Why? What business do you have with him?"

"I want his head. He murdered my father after he did not give Neptune control of our tribe."

"You want to avenge your father too? I'll agree to your conditions. However, I have one ally in my tribe helping me, but we can only meet every two weeks. I agreed to work with Neptune because he promised to cleanse our tribe of the Moon Curse, my sister is pregnant, and I don't want her to die. I want to make sure she's safe."

"All right, you must stay in this tent, away from everyone. You don't believe as we do, so I can't mix you in like that."

"Cove, I was not raised to believe in the Universe, but life is showing me the error in that way. Please give me time to give the Universe a try. I want to believe differently—I want to be different. Give me a chance," Tiber pleaded with the young chief.

"They'll need a form of payment now." Cove extended his hand.

Tiber reached into her bag and gave him her locks of hair. "Hair from my head—plenty of it."

Cove inspected its length and quality. "All right, this should be able to pay for a tent and some new clothes. Give me a while, and I'll be back." Cove left Tiber and Mika isolated in the tent. The panther purred after Cove freed her from the vine entanglement.

"I told you we would be starting over, Mika. Here's my chance to transform into a better person. I just hope that I can clear my name. I don't want my tribe to think I'm a murderer when I know I'm not. I still don't even know what to think about my father's last words to me. Just how much did he know? Did he know about Neptune and his plans for our tribe? Did he know that I was working with Neptune? Mika, I'm scared that my mistakes may have marred Father's last thoughts of me." Tiber began to sob into the soft jet-black pelt. She heard footsteps and quickly wiped her eyes dry. As the tent flap opened, she saw the girl from earlier with two plates of food.

"Eat up, now." She slid one plate of raw meat to Mika and another plate with cooked fish and vegetables to Tiber. "I'll bring you something to drink later." The girl with the paint-clad face turned to leave.

"Rilian, thank you," Tiber called to her.

Rilian turned to face Tiber and nodded slightly before exiting the tent. Shortly after she left, Cove returned with some clothes in hand. "I talked briefly with my council. You will be sharing a tent with one of our tribe sisters for the time being. Here are a few changes of clothes. I must see who will be willing to allow you to stay with them."

"Cove, can I clear my name by having the Seer vouch for me?"

"To be honest, I don't think it's a good idea to go to her first. You almost killed her, accident or not. She overpowered you half-dead. It's not wise. It would be best if you focused on consolidating information about

Neptune so you can convince her that you've changed when you see her. So, this will rest on you and your tribe ally doing their part."

"Thank you, I appreciate the help."

Rilian returned with water jugs. "Oh, I'm sorry." She began to leave.

"Rilian, wait, can Tiber stay with you?" Cove asked.

"Well—for how long?" Rilian raised her thin dark brown eyebrows.

"Let's just start with a month for now, then we can come back and reassess things," Cove suggested.

"All right, I'll try." Rilian gave Tiber one of the water jugs. "I'll take this one back to my tent. I'll come and get you once I've made space."☐

After Rilian left, Cove spoke, "Well, there you go. Rilian can be intense, but she's charming once you get to know her. I think you'll get along well. I'm sorry about your father, Tiber. My father always told me that Chief Dalit was a good man and believed in equality for the tribe's brothers and sisters. He will be greatly missed. I hate to ask this, but do you know who the successor is?"

"No, he did not discuss things like that around my sister or me." Tiber thought hard. "Cove, what kind of work will I start doing? You know, to do my fair share."

"I was thinking about that. I understand that you want to clear your name. We are going to have to move quickly. Once your tribe realizes you are nowhere in their domain, they will start questioning my tribe and Marina's tribe. You must clear your name, but I don't think the Seer will even talk to you after what's happened, so you need to pique her interest and offer her something she can't resist. Your job must be flexible enough to allow you time to travel and gather information. How about this, we will both sleep on it and meet in the morning as I introduce you to a few key tribe members?"

"Okay, I can do that." Tiber nodded.

"All right, well, Rilian should be getting you soon. I must go now, but we'll meet in the morning." Cove left Tiber and Mika in the tent. She thought long and hard about what he said, and he was right. Tiber knew that even attempting to contact Aqila right now could plunge her people straight into a war. A battle between the Windmasters and the Tribe of Snow and Ice was a guaranteed defeat for her people. However, she wasn't sure if she could gather enough information on Neptune to get Aqila's attention. Instead of trying to take her fate into her own hands, she decided that she would be patient and give the Universe a chance to help her.

"Tiber, I've made a spot for you and your panther. Onca won't bother her. I'll be sure of it." Rilian smiled. At this point, it was incredibly dark. How Rilian could navigate surprised Tiber. She would instinctively reach out for her when she felt unsure of her step. In the distance, she could see fire light and hear chanting, but Rilian pulled her in the opposite direction. "Maybe another time. Tonight Cove wants you to get settled."

As they entered her tent, Tiber saw a floor bed set up for her. "Mika, you must stay out here. Everything will be okay." Mika obeyed Tiber and stayed outside. She could tell that Onca, Rilian's jaguar, was several feet away. Tiber put her bag in the corner by the floor bed.

"Do you have any blankets?"

Rilian looked bewildered. "Why do you need blankets? It's the jungle!"

"I'm not cold, but, well, never mind." She turned to face the tent wall. She closed her eyes when she felt Rilian's footsteps approach her. Suddenly, a brisk wind hit Tiber's skin followed by the gentle caress of fabric.

"I don't have blankets, but I've got plenty of sheets. I'm going out now. Try and get some sleep. I won't be gone too long."

The additional layers provided comfort. Tiber wanted to tell her that a blanket would make her feel at home, but she didn't have a home anymore. Her people wanted her dead. Her father was dead, and her sister would die as soon as she had her baby. Tiber fought back the tears. How could she go back if she had no family to return to? She wished she had listened to Aqila's reasoning. Aqila told her that she had no proof that Neptune was who he said he was. She and Nahal were supporting a power-hungry murderer. Then Tiber thought about Sita. She didn't know what was going on. Sita was going to try to get information from Nahal. Her life could be in danger if she got too close to him.

Frustrated with everything, Tiber tossed around on the bed. She tried to think of a plan that would allow her to clear her name. However, the blaring truth was that clearing her name meant exposing Nahal and Neptune. Her tribe was divided; some strongly followed her father and their tribal customs, and the rest were staunch followers of Neptune. If she exposed Nahal, she would be facing the wrath of Neptune himself.

"If I must die for everything I've done, that would only be justice. I betrayed my father's trust, carried out missions in Theyra, attacked and nearly killed a Seer, and was willing to capture the Fireheart Legend. Maybe it's too late for me to get out unscathed. Maybe the price I must pay is death. But if I have to die, I'll die for the crimes I've committed and no one else's," she vowed.

When Tiber's eyes opened again, it was morning. She was disoriented. She didn't remember falling asleep. She moved the sheets and stood up. The tent was rather large. Tiber's bed was toward the front entrance. As she walked further toward the back, she saw a large pot in one area with extra-long skewers and water jugs nearby. This was Rilian's kitchen. There was a flap leading to an outside toilet and wash bowl. After coming back inside, she pressed forward a little more. There were a couple of other rooms before the exit flap. She was knocked over when she turned to go back to her mat.

"Ahh!"

"Why are you shouting? I live here! What are you nosing around for?"

Tiber stood up. "I woke up and was just looking around. You've got a nice place."

"Thanks, I was going to show you around when I came back, but you've taken care of that already." A small smile could be seen underneath the turquoise face paint. "Come on, I'll fix you a proper meal."

Tiber followed Rilian into the kitchen area. She had multiple sacks that were neatly tied. Rilian grabbed bowls from one sack and bread from another before handing a bowl to Tiber. "I'll show you how to make a jam. It only takes a few minutes. You put water in the pot, just enough to cover the bottom. We don't have many places to store food, so I try not to make too much. I put my fresh berries in. Look, not too many. Now, we want to heat it." She looked at Tiber. "I know you know how to light wood. So grab a piece from the front and put it under the pot on this hot iron plate."

Tiber grabbed the piece of wood, some cotton, and wire that Rilian had at the front of the tent and took it outside. After lighting the wood, she carefully placed it on the hot plate, just like she would have done at home. In a couple of minutes, they could hear the water boiling.

"Put some sugar in and mix. It will get thick quickly. After it thickens, you pat the flame out with a wood board. And it's done! Okay, grab the board and pat the flame."

Tiber followed instructions and fanned the smoke that followed the extinguished flame. She peered into the pot and was in awe at the chunky fruit substance. Rilian scooped multiple spoonfuls onto their bread. Tiber tasted, and it was wonderful, warm, and super fruity.

"Mmm, this is so good. How have I lived without this?"

Rilian covered her food-filled mouth as she replied, "Girl, you haven't lived at all."

Tiber smiled at her response. The two ate in peace as a voice called out, "Permission to enter, Rilian."

"Come on in, Cove," she replied.

"Well, it seems like you two are getting along. Rilian, some of the women need some assistance at the river. Also, I need to speak with you, Tiber."

Rilian wiped her mouth with the back of her turquoise-painted hand as she stood. Her vibrant ocean-blue eyes smiled excitedly. "I'll be right there." She immediately headed to the front entrance, and Onca was at her side at once. Rilian mounted and was off, her turquoise paint glimmering in the early morning sun.

"Are you doing okay?"

"Yeah, I'm as fine as I can be with everything going on right now," Tiber replied. Cove sat beside her on the floor.

"I—I know how you feel. My father was taken away from me much too soon. In this tribe, chiefship is passed to the family. Since I'm an only child, everything was left to me."

"When did your father pass?"

"I was nine. My mother raised me in her tribe until I was twelve. The men here helped me become a man my father would have been proud of."

"How do you know that Neptune killed your father? You were so young," Tiber questioned.

"Kano's father taught me the ropes of chieftainship and was standing chief in my stead. He told me how Neptune killed my father. Neptune wanted my father to hand over control of the tribe to him. My father said he could only take the tribe if he won rights through a fair duel. They went to the jungle to duel, each bringing a witness. My father won in a fair fight. When he went to embrace Neptune for a well-fought fight, he stabbed my father in the back with an ice dagger. Kano's father, Yuval, went to help my father. He realized Neptune's witness was a Fireheart. Yuval had several burns on his hands and arms as he tried to help my father. He died instantly. After the murder, Neptune knew the Jungle tribe would never bow to him. He has never made another attempt since."

"That's awful. I'm sorry, and I feel horrible for having supported him."

"Why did you support him? He's nothing but a power-hungry murderer."

"Well, my father supported Neptune's ideas of a united Waterbearer tribe—for all three tribes to become one. Like the Windmasters, one nation with two territories. Neptune promised that he could rid our women of the Moon Curse. My father lost his first wife and my mother to the curse, so he agreed. Neptune didn't ask for control of our tribe. He said he wanted a percentage of our soldiers. The friction came when Neptune started badmouthing my father's decisions to our soldiers, creating a divide in our tribe. My father wanted to see Neptune fulfill his promise at the end of two years. Then, my older sister became pregnant. She and her husband do not have two years, so I started working for him."

"I know you may not want to hear this, but in the past, curses that affected people like that came from disobeying the Universal Order. I know your tribe thinks they have done everything they could, but until they truly repent, the curse won't be lifted. It's happened to people of the past before," Cove explained.

"Everything Aqila said is coming true! Why didn't I listen to her when I had a chance? Then I wouldn't be in this situation."

"That's not important right now because you can't change the past, but you can change now. According to tribal custom, if you don't work, you can't stay here. So, we need to come up with a job for you. I was thinking that maybe you could shadow Rilian, especially since you two seem to be getting along."

"What does Rilian do?"

"She's a vanguard, securing the women and children in their daily duties and responsibilities. Since you could fight on par with her, I thought that job would give you enough flexibility to pursue your mission."

"Thank you so much, Cove. You didn't have to do any of this. I appreciate it, really." Tiber beamed with excitement.

He stood up and headed to the tent entrance. "Anytime. If you need anything, you should ask Rilian, but never hesitate to come to me," he flashed a friendly smile before disappearing from her view.

Tiber sighed. Although she felt like an outsider, she truly believed that the Jungle tribe could begin to feel like home in time. She changed into her new clothes. Her fur clothes barely fit her new form and were impractical for the warmer jungle climate. The teal, long, lightweight skirt was airy with side slits on both sides that came to her knees. Her new top was a pale shade of turquoise with three-quarter-length sleeves. She left to get Mika, who immediately greeted her. The sight of the Jungle tribe was absolutely breathtaking. It was so lush and green. There were tall trees with elaborate canopies all around her. The tribe was busy on the jungle floor and bustling in the treetops. Bridges and tree houses were peppered with canopy greens. This was very different from the icy whites and blues of her home tribe. Thinking of home, she hoped Sita was doing all right with the chaotic state of her tribe.

CHAPTER II

It was another day in the Tribe of Snow and Ice as Sita began her morning routine. All the injured tribesmen had recovered. Unfortunately, none of them could remember anything of the events that occurred over two weeks ago.

"Sita, come quick." Shasa huffed, clearly out of breath and urgently concerned. Sita's steel-blue eyes widened with concern as she hurried to her tribe sister's side.

"What's wrong?"

Shasa's eyes watered. "Sita, it's horrible! Elder Akay has passed. You're needed in the elder tent."

Sita staggered backward. Her heart felt weak. Elder Akay was an esteemed pillar of the community. Having never had children, she lived a long life and was a mother figure to two generations of tribe children. She turned to her lair and prepared the burial mixture as she had done recently for their fallen chief.

Afterward, she carefully headed to Chelan's tent. She silently prayed that no one would catch her. It was utterly inappropriate for a single woman to be seen heading to the tent of a single man who was not engaged to her. Her mind was plagued with these thoughts as she neared Chelan's tent.

"Sita!"

She nearly passed out from surprise. "Nahal, good morning. How are you doing?"

"Sita, you look shocked to see me. Haven't you heard the news about Elder Akay?"

"I have. It's devastating. She was a mother to all of us."

He gripped her shoulders gently, pulling her into an embrace. She felt his chin pressed against her head. "Shouldn't you be preparing her for burial?" She found his gentle tone to be soothing.

Sita sighed, "I know, and I am, but Chelan offered to help me manage my workload until he has redeemed his warrior status. So I was just coming to get him."

Nahal raised his eyebrows. "I'm glad to see that he's working on getting back in good standing. Anyway, I know this is a trying time for the tribe. If you don't mind, I'd like to invite you to dinner with my family to thank you for everything you've done. You've worked tirelessly; I don't want that to be overlooked. You know, I'm more than willing to help with things in the medicine lair."

"You don't have to do that! I mean, I'm just doing my duty. And I'm honored to contribute my skills," Sita replied.

"Hey, Sita—" Chelan started, abruptly stopping when he saw Nahal.

"Good morning. I was just coming to get you. There are a lot of herbal mixtures to restock, and I have something urgent to tend to. I have the instructions posted for you." Sita immediately turned to Chelan, trying to catch his eyes as often as possible.

"Okay, yeah, let me wash up, and I'll meet you." Chelan walked away, genuinely confused.

Nahal's eyes flashed with annoyance before he sighed, "Well, Sita, I'll be enjoying your company at dinner this evening. And be careful. I don't like that Chelan lets his guard down too easily."

Sita noticed the change in his demeanor. "I know that you are still upset about what happened with Chief Dalit. He has had a chance to account. Can we move forward from this? Or is there something else I should be worried about?"

Nahal stopped in his tracks. "No, I don't want you worried about anything. I know I should let things go. It's just hard. We're always losing people, and the entire situation has been weighing on me. I'll get it together, I promise. Now please excuse me. I need to prepare the service for our elder." Sita watched Nahal leave. She felt like she could finally breathe. She hurried back to the lair. She wrote down some notes in case Nahal stopped at the lair and interrogated Chelan while she was away.

Sita watched Nahal return to his tent, probably to prepare for the burial service. Soon afterward, Chelan came jogging toward her.

"You wanna tell me what all of that was about?"

"Be quiet!"

"Sita, what's going on?" Chelan whispered.

"Elder Akay passed away last night. I must go and prepare the body, so I need you to stay here for a while.

How are things between you and Nahal? He seems not to trust you."

"Since I've made my account, he's been hot and cold with me. Speaking of trust, I don't trust him one lick. When I was at your tent, he interrogated and knocked me out. I wanted to tell everyone, but Nahal has gained most of the tribe's trust. However, I knew better than to press my luck."

"I know, w—we talked about it. He's been upset about the chief's death and the whole Tiber situation. I can't help but feel like something else is going on. Either way, I must be on my way." Sita left her lair and hurried to the elder's tent. As she approached closer, Shasa was leaving, breathing heavily, and she was looking unwell.

"Shasa, what are you doing?"

"The tribe sisters helped me take the rest of the elders out for fresh air. I thought it would help take their minds off things," she whispered, her dark blue eyes reflecting only a deep sadness.

Sita gently touched her shoulder. "And yours? I know so much has been going on, and this is a trying time for you. But it will get better. I know it will. No matter what happens, you can't just stop caring for yourself. Why don't you try and get some rest."

"I really need to make the preparations for tonight's dinner."

"I can come over early to help out," Sita offered.

"That would be wonderful. I haven't had any bonding time with the sisters since Tiber."

"I know, and I hardly ever have time to socialize with everything that's been happening lately. So, I am looking forward to our time together. Now, go and rest before I tell Muraco that you are not complying with the healer's orders."

Shasa laughed. "Okay, I'm going! Please don't get him started!"

Sita hurried into the tent. Elder Akay was lying peacefully on her bed. Her eyes were closed, her skin had a grayish hue, all life had slipped away from her. Sita had prepared many bodies for burial. Many mothers gave their lives for their newborns. Many husbands, fathers, and brothers died on fatal hunting expeditions. And most recently, Chief Dalit. None of their deaths hurt like this. Sita never knew her mother, but Elder Akay raised her like a daughter. Akay had been the tribe medic and taught

Sita her craft since she was young. She was so full of love, intuition, and wise lessons. Akay would truly be missed.

Sita wiped her eyes dry and took a deep breath as her body trembled. It was difficult to force herself to start the examination. Squeezing her eyelids shut, she allowed her mind to drift to more comforting thoughts. Locks of dark brown hair and sharp cerulean eyes danced in her memory. Nahal! His charming smile put her at ease.

Wait! What am I thinking?

Sita shook her head free from such thoughts. She started examining the body, and she noticed that Akay's tongue and the inside of her mouth were blue. "What is that?" Sita had never seen anything like this before, but she knew that this was not normal. She knew what she had to do, but the thought of it made her stomach sick. But she had to discover the truth. Sita snipped some of Akay's hair and wrapped it in a small white cloth. Mustering up all of her courage, she held her breath as she did the unthinkable.

Chelan was organizing the herb blends per Sita's instructions when he noticed Nahal exit his tent. The lead guard, Yas stopped him. They were looking at something near the edge of the mountain chain. Muraco appeared from a distance, hauling his hunt behind him. Yas tapped

Nahal's shoulder and tilted his head Muraco's way. The pair ceased talking, and Yas went to the guard's tent. Chelan made himself busy as Nahal approached Muraco. "That was weird," he whispered. He saw Sita leave the elder's tent. She was heading back to the lair. Nahal called out to her, and she walked over to talk to him. Annoyance tugged at Chelan to see Sita and Nahal so familiar with each other. He could not tell if he was more annoyed by Sita being so trusting of him or if it was the natural chemistry between the pair. Finding a spouse in the Tribe of Snow and Ice was a difficult process due to the Moon Curse. Only those with the "best genes" were allowed to marry and have children. It truly was survival of the fittest for the benefit of the tribe. The pair's laughter distracted Chelan from his thoughts.

"Whatever makes her happy."

Sita was jogging toward the medicine lair. Her smile faded as a long sigh escaped her lips.

"You didn't take long," Chelan tried to start a conversation.

"How are the herbs coming along?"

"Well, I finished cleaning the glass jars for the tinctures you told me about, and I'm finishing the tea blends."

"Hey, Chelan, it's nice to see you helping Sita out." Nahal nodded toward the former warrior. "Sita, I hope he's not bothering you too much." Nahal leaned against the icy lair entrance, grinning from ear to ear.

Sita smiled. "Oh, Nahal! Chelan has been a huge help. I think he missed his calling as a tribe medic."

Chelan's midnight blue eyes widen at the compliment, "Thanks, Sita."

"I forgot to ask when we were talking just now, is Elder Akay's body ready for burial? I've planned the service for tomorrow evening."

"That's way too soon. I just examined the body today. The sisters must pick her burial garment and dress her for the service. I also have to plan the ice ceremony. The body will be ready next week," Sita explained.

"I don't see why all of that is necessary. We buried the chief the same evening," Nahal looked slightly confused.

"Yes, the chief burial ritual is completely different. It is a tradition that the chief is buried as soon as possible. Nahal, I must complete the process per our customs."

"I understand. I was not familiar with the process. That seems like a lot of work. I'm trying to consider you too; will you need any extra assistance?"

"I appreciate the concern, but Chelan's help will be enough. You know I intend to perform my job properly and per our tribe's customs."

"Of course, whatever it takes, right? I'll let you get back to it." He smiled and walked away.

Once he was a distance away, Chelan groaned. "I have never seen anyone vying for the chief's spot like him."

Sita was watching Nahal's back when she heard Chelan's comment, "How could you say that? Nahal is doing excellent in the face of so much pressure. Chief Dalit was the chief for our whole lives. The tribe is getting antsy without clear leadership."

"I didn't expect you to jump to his defense. I didn't say that he wasn't doing well at leading the tribe. It's just clear that he is after the position."

"I have no intention of arguing; I have more pressing concerns."

"Like?"

"Solving Elder Akay's murder," Sita whispered.

"What are you talking about?"

"I think she was poisoned."

"Whoa, you can't come with what you *think*. What do you *know*?"

"I know it was not a natural cause. It was not a natural death. Akay was in decent health for her age. She was nearing one hundred years old, but she didn't die of natural causes."

"What are you going to tell everybody? What are you going to tell your Nahal? Do you think he did it?"

"Of course, I don't think he did it. I told him I had examined the body, but he didn't react. His expression never changed. I'm having dinner with Shasa's family tonight, including Nahal and Mahak, so I'll cast a few hooks and see who bites. However, I'm certain none of them were involved."

"Sita, be careful. If you're right, we are dealing with two murders. Now that Elder Akay is dead, you're not a healer anymore. You are *the* tribe medic; we need you. I know you feel strongly that Nahal was not involved, but he never completed his account of the tribe attack. He has something to gain from her death."

"Okay, you two have to stop this! I just told Nahal to let go of the fact that you weren't at your post when the chief was murdered. Now, you let it go! Okay, Nahal punched you and made you look bad, but you are cleared. Stop making him the bad guy."

"Fine. Just make sure that the word travels about having to examine the body. Be certain that the entire tribe knows. Anyone who starts questioning you is an immediate suspect. Let me know who's on your list, and I'll have your back from there."

Sita tapped his arm. "Sounds like a plan, you're starting to sound like the lead warrior. You hold things down here, and I'll get to it."

Chelan wasn't sure what exactly was happening, but Nahal and Yas had an arrangement of some sort. He didn't want Sita to get hurt. Yas was the lead guard. If he's tied up with Nahal, every guard in the tribe could be tied to him. He silently prayed that he was wrong, but if he was right, he only trusted himself to protect Sita. The hunters were under Muraco's leadership, the guards under Yas, and the warriors were under him; except now, he's been removed from duty.

"How are things coming here, Chelan," Shasa's soft voice called to him.

"Everything's going well, thank you. I thought you'd be trying to get some rest."

"I wanted to walk around for a bit. No one's home since Muraco's out hunting. I was looking for Sita."

"She's working on things for the burial, so I'm following her notes here."

"Oh, we had plans to work on the dinner for tonight together. Would you like to join us?"

Chelan thought about Nahal and Sita sitting together, laughing and enjoying the evening. "I appreciate the offer, but I'll pass this time."

Shasa tilted her head. "Well, if you change your mind, you are welcome in our tent anytime."

CHAPTER 12

After a week of living with the Jungle tribe, Tiber was not an official member, but everyone was quite hospitable toward her. She began learning to be a vanguard from Rilian, who was highly proficient with her Element. Tiber felt like the more she learned about water, the more she learned about herself. She could finally do some fighting maneuvers barefoot, like a Jungle tribe woman. It felt weird walking around without her boots. She appreciated her new Jungle tribe clothes, but her preference was still her parka, caribou pants, and boots. In the jungle, the men wore low-cut sleeveless shirts and painted their face, arms, and upper body. The women wore flowy dresses with high slits; if they had sleeves, they were sheer. Everyone walked around barefoot. The ground was wet and soft most of the time, and it took Tiber some time to get used to having damp feet all day.

Today Rilian had to venture outside of the tribe hub. With Rilian gone, Cove planned for them to catch up. Tiber was nervous. She made promises to herself and her people and feared that she wouldn't be able to keep any of them. She was sitting on the floor in the kitchen area of Rilian's tent. She just retrieved the last bit of jam from the bottom of the pot for her bread.

"I hope you saved some for me," Cove remarked as he entered.

"Sorry, you just missed the best part." Tiber smiled back.

"Rilian's going to be out for a while. I thought it would be a good idea to catch you up on things. A few of your tribesmen petitioned me about your whereabouts. I told them I had not heard or seen anything unusual in my tribe. Also, I expressed that I had not seen any evidence of a Snow tribe girl and that if I came across anything, I would inform them. I did tell them that they were free to come and see things for themselves."

Tiber's mouth dropped, her bread nearly falling out.

"It's okay. Calm down, and hear me out. The last time they saw you, you didn't look like this. You look like a woman now. You're dressed in Jungle tribe clothes, so you should be able to blend in. To be quite honest, most of the tribes have intermixed, so all of us to some extent share similar features. So, I don't think it will be a problem if they come through. They won't be able to single you out. I don't want you to be nervous, though. As of right now, your tribe has not accepted my offer to come here. Now, I hope you are not mad at me about this . . . I wrote to Aqila and asked for an audience with her here."

Tiber felt weak. "Why? Did you miss the part where she almost didn't leave Avala with her life? Or maybe you forgot the part where I poisoned her and captured her! Oh, did we even get to the part where this 'Seer' was powerful as icy hell and nearly killed me?"

"Listen! Your sister is still pregnant. You don't have a lot of time! Neptune might have a bounty on your head. Your father is dead, and a new chief could permanently ban you from your tribe. You don't have time to argue with me on this. I know you don't really know me well, but you must trust me. I told Aqila I needed an audience to verify past facts for a tribe member whose life was in danger. Aqila said that she had another equally pressing matter, but she would arrive later in the week. But she also said that she would not be coming alone."

"What does that mean?"

"Well, she's engaged to Kavi, and I received news a week ago that she is officially a full Seer. They'll probably be coming together. You know, romancing. You know how those Windmasters are with their soulmates."

"Am I supposed to know who Kavi is?"

"He's the firstborn son of Ruler Akash and Ruler Sufa of Kashmala."

"She's marrying the son of a ruler? I am dead. You just signed a death sentence for me."

"Tiber, please. I would not have invited them if I thought they would kill you. In that case, I could just tell your tribe that you're here. You're going to have to trust me just a little more. Kavi is the most logical person I know. He's a good man! Big picture, little picture, he gets it. And initiating violence is not the Windmaster way. Everything will be okay. Now, for your part. We can't wait anymore. You must contact your tribe ally, which requires sneaking back in. You won't be alone. Rilian will help you."

"I'll do it. I trust you, Cove. I don't trust myself right now, but I trust you. I trust Rilian, and I know that she has my back. But, what—"

"The worst-case scenario is that your allies have not found anything or got caught. In that case, we need Aqila more than ever. We need her sight to prove something is wrong," Cove reassured her.

"When do we go?"

"This afternoon. You know nighttime is the hub of Waterbearer life. So anyone could spot you at night. Rilian will meet you near the border, and Kano will be several paces behind you the entire time. I told you that we have to give Aqila some information for this to be worthwhile."

"I understand, and I'll be ready."

Cove left Tiber in the tent. It was approaching midday, so she did not have much time to prepare. She wanted to prove to Cove that she trusted him and that he could trust her. He has been there for her when her own tribe shunned her. She was afraid of Aqila coming to the Jungle tribe with her fiancé. She was fearful of crossing paths with her. Tiber shivered, remembering those angry silver eyes gazing into hers. It felt like she was being suffocated. And the worst of it was that she pushed Aqila to that point. Everything

Aqila mentioned had been true, especially about Neptune and even the things she said about the Universe. It scared Tiber to believe in the Universe. She was slowly trying to open up to the fact that the Universe was powerful and could bless and protect.

She rode Mika into the tribe grounds, walking among the jungle brush. Everyone was so kind to her. Women and children occupied this part of the village. Some women cooked together, while others gathered water and washed clothes. In the distance, it was school time for the children. Closer to the river, water classes were being held, training the tribe members in fighting techniques.

Tiber never knew how resourceful the Jungle tribe was. Most of its members could pull water from other sources or manipulate water within a source. It made sense, seeing how lush the jungle stayed. She noticed that each tribe had a slightly different style and proficiency. In her tribe, turning water into ice and snow was necessary, and vice versa. This strategy required the development of pinpoint precision. The Jungle tribe lacked the elegance of form. However, their fluidity and resourcefulness were advantageous. Due to the skill level needed to be productive, this tribe was physically the strongest and most adaptable tribe. The Beach tribe was the most graceful. Their fighting stemmed purely from tribal dance. They could move large amounts of water effortlessly while utilizing other techniques, increasing their power level.

It was indeed a perk to trade techniques with Rilian, and Tiber saw the results—her proficiency with water expanded, having been here for only one week. Tiber realized her elemental appetite increased after her Changing. She felt more hungry and powerful. She just had not had the chance to explore her ability thoroughly.

Lost in thought, she had not noticed that Mika had stopped. Tiber was close to the school, and one of the young schoolgirls was giving Mika some attention. She had a fish enclosed in a ball of water.

"I just want to give her a fishy." The child smiled apprehensively. She had rich brown skin with cool undertones that emphasized her bright blue eyes.

Hmmm, she must have some Beach tribe blood with eyes like that.

Tiber patted her cat's flank. "Open, Mika." The cat obeyed and ate the fish the child had offered.

"Yay! Thank you! I wanted to feed your cat the first day I saw her. Hi Mika." The child roughly petted Mika, much to the leopard's annoyance. Mika spit the water from the girl's fish-filled ball into her face.

"Mika!" Tiber groaned.

The child laughed. "It's okay. I'm sorry I made you eat all that water, Mika." The girl's brown curls were a mess all over her face.

"Luana, what are you doing?" A young woman hurried over to the child. "I'm sorry about her behavior, Tiber."

"No harm done, Anahita." Tiber smiled at Luana's mother.

"If you say. Well, I hope you come by the sisters' tent to pick some clothes for the summer festival."

"The festival . . . I—I well—"

"Come on, Tiber, it only comes around once a year. At first, I thought you were here because you had married one of the tribe brothers. Since that's not the case, you should enjoy the festival. That is what it is for—bringing tribes together. If you decide to go, please come by the sisters' tent. Luana, stop playing with Mika. I have to get you cleaned up." Anahita waved as she marched Luana toward the river.

"Tiber, it is about time we leave," boomed a voice behind her. It was Kano. She barely recognized him without his tribal paint on.

"Yes, I'm ready."

"Cove wants you to see him upon your return."

Tiber nodded and signaled for Mika to go. The leopard seemed to miss her old life of running free and hunting in the wild cold of the mountains. Tiber hoped they were not moving too fast for Kano. Her mind was running with ideas of how she could get Sita's attention. The solidity of her plans was slowly replacing her fears. She decided to take a leap of faith and pray to the Universe that things would work out. Cove kept urging her to trust him earlier, and she did. Tiber decided the only way she could trust herself was to forgive herself. Putting faith in the Universe was helping her heal both her broken heart and wounded pride.

Tribal pride was a significant factor for Waterbearers. Without a tribe, one was lost. Tiber was beginning to feel more torn than lost. She made new friends and allies in another tribe but left her loving sister back home. A part of her wanted to embrace her new life and call the Jungle tribe home. However, she would never be at peace with that until she cleansed her tribe of its afflictions and saved it as her father asked. This was the last quest he asked her to fulfill: save her tribe. Tiber vowed to Father, herself, the moon, and the Universe that she would save them or die trying.

"Easy, princess, you're about to run in face first." Rilian splashed Mika with water, causing the leopard to unsheathe its claws.

"Sorry, I was preoccupied." Tiber dismounted. "I have a plan. We are going to go straight in and talk to Sita."

"Okay, that sounds great." Rilian rolled her eyes. "Now, how are we going to just walk in?"

"Let me get some of that paint." Tiber wiped Rilian's forehead, applying the turquoise paint to her cheeks. "Let's grab some berries and plant leaves. We will act like we are healers in training, and we want to exchange this stuff for some of Sita's supplies."

"Oh, that actually makes sense. You've recently changed, so you don't look the same to them anymore. But will this Sita girl recognize you?"

"Yes, she will. I know she'll recognize me. And Mika having changed in appearance also helps tremendously."

"Shh, someone's over there." Rilian pulled Tiber back several feet. Someone was walking near the icy river. They appeared to be filtering water from the river.

"Tiber, I thought your medic was a girl," Rilian whispered.

"I can't tell who that is right now," Tiber whispered.

The man looked up and turned toward the pair hiding in the thick brush of the border hundreds of yards off. The man came running toward them. Could he see them? Rilian and Tiber steadied themselves in a fighting position. The man was running then came to an abrupt halt as he was a mere few feet from them.

"Who's there?"

Tiber peeked out slowly. "Chelan?"

"Who are you?"

"I'm a healer in training, and we came to get herbs from Sita," Tiber lied. Rilian slowly came out from the brush, followed by Mika and Onca.

"Go back in the brush." Chelan looked around. "Hurry, for your safety."

Tiber and Rilian quickly went back. Chelan again looked toward the mountain before joining them.

"Really, Tiber? What are you doing here?"

"How did you know it was me?"

"Why the icy hell would a Jungle tribe healer know me by name, hmm? Sita isn't available, and you shouldn't come back here without being more careful. Everything here has changed."

"What's happening?"

"I can't be seen because I've been temporarily relieved from my post. Nahal set me up and was going to charge me with being an accomplice in your father's murder. Sita got me off, so I'm helping her until my status is cleared."

"How can Nahal do that? He's not chief," Tiber protested.

"He might be soon. Your father's decree is missing, so we don't know who he chose to succeed him as chief. And tribe custom is that after thirty-one days, the tribe has to vote on a new chief. Nahal has been taking charge, and a lot of people like him and feel safe under his leadership. Don't be surprised if he's voted in. Sita is having dinner with Nahal tonight."

"What!"

"Shut it!" Chelan hushed her. "She's having dinner with your family: Shasa, Muraco, Mahak, and Nahal.

Today, Elder Akay passed away. When Sita examined the body, she said that the death was not from natural causes."

Rilian's eyes went wide, "An elder was murdered?"

Chelan shook his head. "Sita has evidence. It was disgusting."

"What kind of evidence?" Tiber asked.

Chelan looked sick. "Hair and skin samples, then she had to cut a piece of her tongue because it was blue. I almost threw up when she told me. We are investigating the murder of Akay and trying to get something on Nahal. She won't get anything until after dinner."

"Chelan, is there anything else? I mean anything, even if it doesn't seem important."

"Well, I don't know if this means anything, but today, I saw Yas and Nahal seeming to be collaborating on something. They were trying to discuss something, but when Muraco got close, they stopped like they didn't want him to hear what they were talking about. Nahal has also been handing over control of various tasks to Yas."

"Wait, Yas is Nahal's uncle. Isn't he the lead guard?"

"Yes, and since the attack, I have lent Yas half of my warriors. I was planning on getting information from them."

"My father was murdered, but I didn't kill him. Now Akay has been murdered. Chelan, please be careful and watch out for Sita. How's Shasa?"

"To be quite honest, she looks horrible. She's sad and lonely, but the sisters are trying to keep her spirits up. Tiber, I never believed that you killed your father. Nahal is a master manipulator. It's like he speaks, and people listen. I'll be careful and don't worry about Sita. As the lead warrior, I trust her safety to no one other than me. I must go back now, but take care." He turned to leave. "Hey, why don't we try to catch up at the summer festival? We're all single. We can try to get whatever we can and fill you in."

"The festival it is," Tiber reluctantly agreed.

Chelan looked back for a moment. "Maybe I'm wrong about Nahal. I just can't trust him. Something just doesn't feel right. Sita seems to trust him . . . I'm probably overreacting." Chelan left and hurried back to filter water from the icy, cold river.

Tiber grimaced, Rilian touched her shoulder. "Let's get back. You have to fill Cove in."

"This is all—" Tiber started.

"Don't you dare finish that sentence," Rilian interrupted. "I don't know everything that happened, but you are here now trying to set the record straight. Focus on what you can do, believe in the Universe, and the stars will always fall in place. Let's go." Rilian wiped Tiber's teary eyes and led the way. After meeting up with Kano, they quickly rode their respective cats back to the Jungle tribe.

Rilian and Kano went their way, and Tiber led Mika upward to the treetops. She sulked all the way to Rilian's tent. Sadness encased her soul as she entered. All she could think about was her sister, her friends, and the hell Nahal was forging for them. She was angry. She wanted to find Neptune, take his head, and serve it to Nahal firsthand.

"Why the heck is it so cold in here?"

"I'm sorry, Cove," Tiber murmured. She hadn't realized that she was making the room icy.

"I saw you come back. I was about to eat but decided to see how things went." He waited for her reply. "Not good, apparently. Why don't you tell me about it?" He sat with his legs folded on the wooden floor.

Tiber wanted to talk, but tears fell instead. She collapsed, hugging her knees, and sobbed. Cove scooted close to her and embraced her.

"It's all my fault. Things are becoming hell for them, and it is because of me." Tiber cried into his chest.

"Shh, don't say that."

"It's true."

"No, it is not. If it were true, you would not be here."

Tiber pulled away from him and wiped her eyes. Cove turned her head to face him. "Talk to me."

"I couldn't talk to Sita. But she found someone to help her. He told me that he got in trouble after I left. Nahal thought he helped me kill my father. Sita got him off, so he's been helping her. My father's decree is missing, so the tribe doesn't have a chief. They have thirty-one days to choose a chief, and Nahal is trying to win their votes. The worst part is that he's winning them over. He has help. His uncle Yas is plotting something with him, but no one knows what it is. Then there was a murder of an elder. She was the tribe's Moonsayer, making things worse for them. And my sister, she is sick, sad, and lonely."

"I know it's a lot to take in at once. There's a scenario that I know you do not want to hear, but I have to ask. What if Nahal really does believe that you killed your father? At what point did he see you?"

"My father was on the ground, and there was a lot of blood. He had already given me his final wish. I was crying his name around the time Nahal walked in," Tiber reflected.

"If you were to disagree with Nahal, how would he respond?"

Tiber rolled her eyes, "He'd be skeptical. He's not easy to convince of anything."

"Well, that might be a part of it. He really might believe that you are guilty. If he believes that, he will work to convince others of his point of view."

"I almost forgot. Chelan wants to meet up at the summer festival to exchange information."

"Is Chelan Sita's friend you were talking about?"

"Yes, but I would rather not go to the festival."

"Why? It's a cultural tradition. You're a single woman, and it's a good opportunity to meet your future husband."

"I would have gone with my father. He would have introduced me to suitors, and I can't imagine going to meet people without him."

"You could go with me, that is, if you trust me. I'm single, so it should not be a problem." Cove was so relaxed as he suggested that they go together.

Tiber's navy eyes met his teal ones. Moments passed, and her heart was racing. She didn't know what to say. Her mouth was dry, and her throat felt small. "I want to go with you." As the words left her mouth, Tiber shocked herself.

Cove smiled. "Since I'm chief, I don't normally get a chance to go out and enjoy myself. I'd love to go with you." He shook his head feverishly. "Since that's settled, we will give Aqila and Kavi a chance to give their opinion and prepare to meet your people in about a week." He stood up and offered his hand to Tiber. After helping her up, he started to leave.

"I'm starting to believe now . . . in the Universe. It hasn't been easy all the time."

"Becoming someone new is never easy."

"And I trust you, Cove."

He chuckled. "I know. I never thought that you didn't. But you didn't trust yourself enough to let me help you. Now, we are past that. Why don't you join everyone for dinner as a woman of the Jungle tribe?"

Tiber smiled. "I'd like that."

CHAPTER 13

"Aqila, I hope this was a good idea." Jai groaned.

"Good idea or not, it must be done. Do you really want another problem on your hands?" Boaz questioned.

"Come on, stop putting so much negativity into the atmosphere. We don't know what will come of this meeting. Let's agree to be open-minded. Besides, we have plenty of time to deal with problems later," Aqila reminded them as they walked through Upper Ember. Jai had hair covering his face, so his eyes were not so noticeable. Boaz was wearing a burgundy vest, black pants, and boots to better blend in as a Fireheart. His muscular frame was on display as he walked with his arms folded.

The town was bustling and well-developed. Tall buildings made of red brick or gray stone on neatly manicured grass flanked both sides of the cobblestone pathways. It was hard to stick together amid the crowd. Aqila had sent Talon hunting so the massive owl would not draw too much attention to them. They walked until they reached a brick building with a wooden sign painted in bold colors that read "Fiery Cafe."

"Why are we coming here? Are you hungry? Thirsty?"

"No, Bo. Sitara intercepts messages here," Aqila whispered to her long-time friend. The smell of coffee, freshly baked bread, and pastries made Jai and Boaz's stomachs growl as they entered the cafe.

"Go ahead and get something to eat while I ask around." Aqila giggled.

The cafe was half filled with customers. When Boaz and Jai arrived, the girl working at the cash counter had just bagged an order.

"May I get you something?"

Jai turned sideways so she wouldn't catch his eyes, and Boaz stood in front. "A double order of muffins and coffee."

"Espresso muffin and black coffee, piping hot," Jai added.

"Coming right up," she chirped. Excitement filled her light brown eyes as she turned to fulfill their order.

Several minutes passed before Aqila plopped down beside them. "Just a bunch of people asking for insights and visions." She turned her attention to the bagged orders.

"Well, it's not every day *the Seer* drops in," Boaz replied.

"Um, excuse me. How long do orders wait before they are picked up?"

The girl was stirring coffee. "It will not take much longer than ten or fifteen minutes. Customers can place their orders early, and I'll make their bags before they are due to come back."

"Okay, I'll remember that for next time," Aqila murmured. Boaz and Jai paid little attention to her inquiry until she said, "Nice to see you again, Cahya."

Jai almost spit his coffee on Boaz as he looked over in Aqila's direction.

"What do you want?" Cahya seemed irritated.

"To catch up, that's all," she replied calmly.

Cahya snatched his bag. "Yeah, right, with two bodyguards? I'm so convinced."

"Let me remind you that I don't need bodyguards."

"That's not how it sounded when you were in Avala," Cahya spat. Aqila stood so fast that the stool she was sitting on tumbled to the floor.

"Easy," Boaz muttered through gritted teeth.

"You want a demonstration of what happened in Avala?" A violent, whistling wind could be heard outside, followed by crashing thunder. She glared into Cahya's eyes until he took a couple of steps back.

Cahya averted her piercing gaze. "What do you want, Storm?"

"We need to talk," Boaz chimed.

"Cahya, don't make this harder for everyone, including yourself," Jai urged while holding his head down.

Cahya huffed. "Meet me at the border of Upper and Lower, the ruins where we fought Agni. We can talk there." He opened his bag and began eating a bagel as he left.

After he left, Aqila walked outside. Boaz paid for their food and drink with a few coins as they hurried after her.

"You know he didn't really mean any harm." Jai touched her shoulder.

"I know, but that's not an excuse to be rude. It is not in my nature to let people talk down to me."

"I agree, but is it safe for Jai to come with us?" Boaz raised a thick eyebrow.

"Come on, I can hold my own if necessary. And somebody has to fill Arrow in," Jai replied.

"Yes, I know it is risky meeting there. However, we are trying to establish trust between Arrow and Cahya. That cannot be done without Jai. Let's head there now. Jai, how's Arrow?"

"He's doing okay, I guess. The Flamethrowers are a little confused about where things are going, though."

Aqila raised a gray eyebrow, "Why?"

"Well, Yuuna has been holding down the fort since Arrow still seems confused from time to time. We brought Zay back as we last discussed, and the meeting went well. Alena was instrumental in getting him on our side. But after a week, Arrow announced that he would train Zay to be his second-in-command."

"Over Yuuna?" Boaz was shocked.

"Yes, that has the Flamethrowers really uneasy right now."

"He's the leader," Aqila said with assurance. "They should not be uneasy with his decision. And from what everyone has told me, Zay is an incredible asset to the team. He may not have an Element, but it doesn't make him any less valuable. Besides, it will increase his loyalty to the Flamethrowers if he truly feels like an essential piece of the organization. The question is, how did Yuuna receive the news?"

"She was obviously hurt, but she's supporting Arrow all the way."

"What do you think, Jai?" Boaz asked.

"Honestly, I've been trying to stay out of things. I don't want to say anything while still learning how they operate. I don't want them all to side with me because I'm a Legend. I believe Yuuna should have an equal chance to be second-in-command if she wants the position. I agree with you, Aqila, about Zay, but I feel like Arrow should explain what he's after with his decision."

Cahya appeared from near the rubbish on the border.

"I know that you're working on something—"

"And you want to run and tell Arrow all about it, right, Aqila? Well, forget it!"

"No, if it is something that doesn't involve Arrow, I don't see why he would need to know about it. I am a Seer. I know how to keep things confidential. Cahya, I understand that this is a difficult time for you. However, the Flamethrowers are truly worried about you. Are you planning to ever rejoin them?"

"That chapter of my life is complete. I'm not going back there."

"What about Calida?" Jai asked, looking bewildered.

"Calida fulfilled her purpose. She lived her life to the best of her ability. She gave the world all she had to offer. She was brave, she was strong, and her heart was made of pure gold. However, we both knew that we had two different ideas about the direction the Flamethrowers should go." Cahya continued walking through the rubble.

"Calida was the oldest. Father taught her the organization's details, the mission's rise, fall, and resurgence. Me? I'm all about the art. To be a great Fireheart is my destiny. I'm a master with the Element and have been for a long time. After my father passed, our mother started working undercover to get as much information as possible about the next Legend. Father passed the job of rebuilding the Flamethrowers to Calida. That was her life mission: to keep Father's legacy alive.

"She accomplished that, and I will forever be proud of her. Father wanted that from her, but he wanted me to maximize my potential to mend the bond between the two Embers. So, I'm on my own mission. I never wanted to be second-in-command or the leader. I was shocked by Calida's judgment to have Arrow lead despite knowing that he was a royal Pyrocean. However, I'm starting something new in my father's honor."

"What will this place be?" Boaz asked.

"I'm starting a group to protect all of Ember with the hopes that we can once again become one. They will be called the Phoenix Riders," Cahya spoke with pride.

Jai's ears perked when he heard Cahya speaking of a united Ember.

"I will teach them how to turn their willpower into fire; that is what makes the phoenix. It is a manifestation of your own will. The Phoenix Riders will restore true freedom, justice, and equality to the Firehearts of Ember. Then we can stand with pride among the Firehearts of

Pyroc and Kindle. My family's legacy will not be forgotten but will carve its mark in Ember."

"I'm proud of you, Cahya. This is an honorable mission, and you have my full support. I understand what it is like to have a unique destiny. Is this something that you would rather keep from Arrow?" Aqila asked.

"I'm not ready to deal with his questions or one-dimensional viewpoint. I'm not against him at all, don't get me wrong. But, for a long time, I've put my dreams on hold to support my sister's goals and objectives. She gave him the leadership ring, which gave me freedom—freedom to answer the call of destiny. Ember is falling. A cult leader like Agni was able to convince all of these people. We saw what he built—an entire town for everyone who would follow him. Of course, they would. I want our people to see another way, and I will gladly give my life to pave a better path."

"Do you think the people will listen? Don't you think this would attract some backlash from Agni?" Jai asked.

"The Phoenix Riders can help you take down Agni and slow his recruitment process. This way, the Flamethrowers can fulfill their intended purpose, which is to be used as the personal army for the Golden Eyed Legend. After we take down Agni, I want the Phoenix Riders to dissolve the gap in the quality of life between Lower and Upper Ember. Once the quality of life is near equal, they will not resist becoming Ember again. We just have to help our people see the end goal."

"I know I'm not Jai or Aqila, but I want to help however I can," Boaz said.

"Thanks. Now, if you don't mind, I have work to do." Cahya nodded and hurried off into a cloud of smoke.

As he disappeared, Jai sighed, "Arrow is not going to be thrilled to hear this."

"I understand what he's trying to do, and we shouldn't interfere," Boaz warned.

"I agree," said Aqila, "Cahya is bound to do great things. He's a master Fireheart and an excellent teacher. The Flamethrowers need him as an ally, so it would be unwise to disturb him and his work. We should talk to Arrow and persuade him to stop pursuing Cahya. Also, I need to talk to you about something as well."

Jai and Boaz immediately turned to Aqila. Jai scratched his head, "What's up?"

"The Jungle tribe has summoned me to settle a situation, but my mind's eye tells me there is something more to what's happening. I don't normally feel uneasy about providing insight, but this time I do. Plus, someone is tailing me."

"What?" Boaz nearly shouted in astonishment. "Aqila, why are you just now saying something? We've got Jai and you out here in the open with someone essential hunting you down?"

"I just became sure of it. I don't like dealing with anything other than facts, and I didn't want to get you worked up for nothing." She whistled to summon Talon. "Someone went to my house unannounced and went through some of my things. When I went to get Boaz, I noticed a winged shadow when entering the library and again when we went inside the cafe."

Boaz and Jai both strained their necks upward; their eyes searched the sky for anything unusual.

"Like you said, Aqila, let's not get worked up about it. Let's fill Arrow in on everything and plan to go to the Jungle tribe together—the three of us. That way, we'll be safe. We can't go wrong with a Legend, Seer, and Landkeeper. Besides, this could be our lead to discovering something about Neptune," Jai suggested.

"My thoughts exactly," Aqila chimed.

"I think we should split up a bit, especially since someone is tailing Aqila. Jai, are you okay with traveling through Ember alone? I think Aqila and I should ride through Pyroc and land Talon on the Pyrocean border, just to be safe."

"I'm fine walking through town. You two just watch out."

Talon landed near Aqila and squawked. Boaz and Aqila flew off, leaving Jai alone. Walking past the rubbish into Lower Ember, he still had lingering memories of their battle there. His body shuddered. The pain of losing friends in this very spot was likened to being hit by lightning. He wanted nothing more than to end Agni, and if Neptune was mixed up in this business, then he had to go too.

Flying between the clouds, Boaz was curious. "Aqila, does Kavi know that someone is tailing you? Does he know that someone intruded on your personal property?"

"No, things have been so hectic back at home that we decided to push back the wedding date. Our mothers were disappointed about that. We are looking for a home to settle into that's not on the Capitol estate. In the meantime, Windmasters have been visiting Zeroun's mountain home, where I'm living now, asking for insights. Kavi and I are planning an engagement gala to keep our families happy. It's just been so much."

"It sounds like a lot, but he would still want to know."

Aqila sighed, "I'm fully aware of that. Honestly, I don't want to give them any more bad news. This is a huge step. And marrying Kavi, of all people in the entire country of Windmasters, is the most wonderful and stressful thing ever. He will be a ruler, bearing the weight of Kashmala on his shoulders. I'm going to be his wife, but I already have a duty to my people as a Seer and a Legend. If I can't carry my own weight, how can I be the best wife possible to him?"

"Aqila, you love him. That is what makes you the best woman to be his wife. You love him with nothing but pure intentions. I know that in your constantly racing Windmaster mind, a simple answer is a nightmare. But it is just that simple. You want to marry him because you love him. You're stressing over this because you're trying to prove something to yourself that has already been proven."

Aqila smiled, "I guess I'm overthinking things."

"Yeah, you are," Boaz admitted to his friend. "But since he doesn't know, Jai and I will have your back."

"Thanks," Aqila sighed, leaning back into the ride a little bit.

CHAPTER 14

In town, Jai paced himself. He knew that Arrow would be anxious to hear Cahya's answer, but there was a wave of peace coursing through him as he inhaled the light smoke smell of his hometown. The wave of nostalgia made the hairs on the back of his neck stand up. He never thought he would ever place the soles of his feet on his hometown soil again, not after fleeing for his life.

Since receiving the antidote from Aqila, a large portion of the fog that clouded his mind for years had lifted. He vaguely remembered the sandy dunes of Kindle. He could remember the comforting feeling of a father's warm embrace. The echoes of a hearty laugh danced through his mind. He scoured his mind but could never recall an inkling of a mother. After grasping some of the pieces of this elaborate puzzle, Jai felt starved for more. He burned with the desire to reunite with his family. He had many questions for them. He wondered if they ever stopped looking for him and if they knew he was a Legend. He wondered if they had even survived all the turmoil that defined Upper and Lower Ember.

There was a surging need for closure, but he would not tell anyone this. Jai didn't want to be distracted by anything; he could not afford it. Agni was his mission, and stopping him was his destiny.

The Universe was with him. He knew it. He was not alone. He and Aqila made a fantastic team. The Flamethrowers stood on their side, and Cahya supported them. Everything was falling into place. So he wanted to convince himself. There was a question burning in the back of his mind: *What about the other two?* Where were the Legends to represent the Landkeepers and Waterbearers? This was something he and Aqila never talked about—the other two. Did she know? No, she couldn't. She just found out that she was a Legend herself. But maybe she could find out. Jai was embedded in thought as his shoulder connected with someone else's, which had a staggering impact.

"Oh, I'm sorry, forgive me," Jai spoke, quickly brushing his hair in front of his eyes to hide their golden hue.

"It's all right. We both could have been paying a little more attention to the road. This town is not as lively as the upper part of Ember."

"I guess not, but every town has its own charm, wouldn't you say?"

The man chuckled. His light brown eyes glistened in the sunlight. "An optimist? I'm not sure I'd call this charm. But there's nothing wrong with looking for light when you are shrouded in darkness."

Jai's mind buzzed, and he reactively grabbed the man's arm.

He chuckled again. "Have we met before?"

"I—I'm not sure. I mean . . . probably not."

The older man tilted his head. "You're a strong and handsome young man. Do you have a family?"

"No . . . I don't."

"That's a shame. I must say, it's amazing you can see anything with all of that hair in your eyes."

Jai laughed. "What can I say? Do you have a family?"

"I do. It's just me and my wife now, but I had a son once."

Jai's breathing hitched.

He had a son?

It took every fiber of self-control for Jai to refrain from questioning the man.

"I must get on my way; it was nice to meet you, young man."

"Same," Jai whispered. He watched as the distance between them grew larger. His curly black hair danced in the wind behind him. "How old would he be?"

The man slowed to a stop. Turning with a perplexed look, he answered, "About twenty. Is there something I'm missing here? We're strangers, and you are asking a lot of personal questions."

Moving as if he was possessed, Jai walked forward. Once the pair were face to face, he slowly moved the hair away from his golden eyes.

"J—Jai?" The man's eyes widened in disbelief as his gaze met Jai's.

"Yes, it's me." His hands trembled as he pointed to himself.

The man embraced him. Jai struggled to breathe. His heart was pounding. There was a burning in his heart that he could not ignore—the desire to belong to someone, to be with someone, to have a family, to be a part of a family.

Staggering backward, Jai stammered, "Are you m—my father?" The recognition transcended his memory, reaching into the depths of his soul.

"Yes, I'm Yuuta—your father." He touched Jai's face before tugging him into another warm embrace.

A wave of emotions washed over Jai—confusion, longing, and a profound sense of belonging. Though his memories remained elusive, there was an undeniable connection between them. That dark cloud that constantly plagued his brain, was beginning to fade.

Yuuta chuckled deeply. "Those unmistakable golden eyes." Sighing deeply, he roughed Jai's hair over his eyes again. "You must be careful. People here don't believe in the Universe. You shouldn't be seen here."

"But how will I find you again?"

"I live in Comet Town in Upper Ember. Ask for Yuuta, and someone will point the way. But you can't stay here. Jai, my son. Be careful. Your mother would be elated to see you. She'd be so relieved to know you are safe."

"Mother," Jai whispered.

Yuuta touched Jai's shoulder. "I'll save that for another time when you can come and visit."

He inhaled, and the gentle smell of candle wax tickled Jai's nose. His heart desired to go with his father. However, he was right, Jai knew he had to keep his cover. Yuuta tapped Jai's shoulder, releasing a long sigh before reluctantly walking away.

Jai's feet felt plastered to the earth as he just watched his father's silhouette disappear into the crowd of people. He found his hand reaching out, almost fearing that he would not find his father again. He wished that he'd found the courage to ask his father to take him with him. However, within his heart, he knew that was not possible. Agni wanted Jai dead, and he refused to put anyone in unnecessary danger, especially his own family.

After the initial shock of their reunion subsided, a whirlwind of emotions swirled within his mind. Jai's heart felt heavy with the weight of the unknown, and the void left by years of separation was now filled with a mixture of confusion and longing. With each passing moment, fragments of memories teased the edges of his consciousness, only to slip away like wisps of smoke when he tried to grasp them. It was as if his past lay just beyond his reach, tantalizingly close yet frustratingly elusive. Jai shook his head free from the confusion, remembering that Aqila and Boaz would be worried if he didn't hurry and meet them in the forest.

I won't forget him. I promise.

CHAPTER 15

In the forest, several yards from the cabin, Arrow heaved a long sigh. The news of Cahya surprised him. "I understand. I didn't expect this. I never once suspected that he was dissatisfied."

"Well, I wouldn't say that he was dissatisfied. He just had another calling: his own destiny. You have an ally in him and his Phoenix Riders. If I were you, I would keep it that way," Jai replied.

"But Calida would never hold him back from his own calling." Arrow was confused.

"I don't think she was holding him back. However, they went through something tragic with the loss of their father. Cahya did his best to support Calida's transition into leadership; they cleaved to each other. Besides, we know it would have been even more difficult for him to come back here now that she is gone," Aqila explained.

Arrow dropped his gaze. "I suppose you're right."

Aqila cleared her throat. "Well, if we've come to a complete understanding that Cahya is no longer a member of the Flamethrowers, it's settled. Arrow, do you have a moment?"

"Yeah, of course." He absentmindedly shrugged. Jai entered the cabin. With Boaz keeping Talon company, it was just Arrow and Aqila.

"Arrow, what are your goals for the Flamethrowers? I see that you are trying to keep things as Calida had them, but you should have goals you want the team to focus on and objectives for them to meet. If not, your leadership will feel confusing to your team."

"There are things that we need, like recruits and supplies. I'm staying on top of that. Besides that, I want them to learn what it takes to keep things running. If I had died too, the Flamethrowers would be up the creek, especially with Cahya gone. No one knows how to operate this organization other than me right now, and I see that as a vulnerability. I have been pushing them to learn the ins and outs and do tasks without me, but I'm not sure if it is clicking."

"Have you told them that this is what you want?"

"Not really, but I don't think it's hard."

"Is there a reason why you didn't choose Yuuna for second-in-command?"

"Of course there's a reason. I didn't choose Yuuna because we are both Pyroccans, and I don't want them to feel like I chose her because of that. Yuuna and I have known each other for a long time. She was the first person I recruited. I trust her with my life. However, I am not trying to replicate the feeling of a royal family or anything. With Zay coming in, I thought it would be an excellent opportunity to show him that we trust him. He's just as strong and smart as anyone else. Not having an Element should not be a barrier to advancement."

"I'll be transparent. The Flamethrowers are a little uneasy about how you've been doing things. If you let them know your motives, it would help clear the air. They started thinking you were doing things differently because your judgment was clouded."

"No, my judgment is not clouded. I always have a lot on my mind, but I'm managing, and every day, it gets better. I guess I've been so worried about saying something wrong that I haven't been communicating at all."

"Take it from someone who has also lost someone close to her. Talking about it brings peace. Running from what feels real will always leave you in pieces."

"Calida's last words to me were not to fear anything that reminded me of her. I should talk to Yuuna so she understands. We've practically grown up together. Sometimes, I can talk to her just like I'm talking with you; then, there are times when I don't feel I'm emotionally available to talk to her."

"I know it's hard. It still doesn't seem real that Zeroun isn't waiting for me with new lessons, assignments, and insights. However, you learn what love and trust are when you give those close to you a glimpse of your vulnerabilities, and they fight to protect them."

"Do you really understand? I—I ruined their lives. I ruined Yuuna's life. Yet she is still here, trusting and supporting me. I loved Calida, but I failed to protect her when she needed it most. I failed everyone that I have ever loved: my family, my people, the Flamethrowers. If Sheraga had been fighting Agni, he would have won. My best is never good enough, especially when people need me."

Aqila gently placed her hand on his shoulder. "I do understand. You'll never be Sheraga, like I'll never be Zeroun. There's only one Sheraga, and there was only one Zeroun. There's only one Arrow and one Aqila. We are who we are, and our best gets better. We fail, and we learn from those failures, and we get better. The Arrow that is here today is to pave the way for a greater version of yourself tomorrow."

"Thanks . . . I needed that. I'm taking your advice and will update everyone tonight." Arrow took a deep breath. "So, where are you headed?"

"I'm going to the Jungle tribe. Chief Cove asked for insight into an urgent matter. Jai and Boaz are coming with me."

"This could lead to some information on Neptune. Are you sure you don't want to wait until tomorrow and take some of the Flamethrowers with you?"

"No, we should be fine, but thank you." The pair headed inside the cabin. Arrow immediately left to talk to Yuuna while Aqila looked for Jai. She saw him talking with Arin, Alena, and Zay.

"Jai, are you ready?"

"I'll be right back," he spoke to the Flamethrowers before following Aqila outside.

"Aqila, I won't be able to go with you this time. Something rather important has come up. You'll be okay with Boaz, right? Or can I meet you there?"

"Well, if something urgent has come up, maybe we can help you—"

"No, that's not necessary. Just trust me on this one." Jai was unsure of what Aqila would say. Her silver eyes were piercing. He almost felt the need to look away from her.

"Of course, Jai, whatever you need. If you believe this to be best, Boaz and I will proceed with our journey. If something develops and you're needed, we'll send word." Aqila left Jai at the cabin and headed in the direction of Boaz. The uneasy feeling may not have come from her meeting in the Jungle tribe but from Jai. Aqila scoured her mind's eye, but there was nothing. That was unusual, as it had not happened since becoming a full Seer. She scoured again.

Not yet, Aqila. If you could see everything whenever you wanted, you'd be a god. The sight is about balancing truth and timing. She heard Emet's voice.

I've never felt someone lie to me like that. I thought Jai trusted me.

You're still getting used to your Seer abilities. Like I said, you must learn balance.

So, you are saying that either I don't have enough information, or the timing isn't right?

Or it is not for you to know. That is possible too. Seer does not mean all-knowing.

"Yes, it is possible," she whispered. Boaz was waiting beside Talon.

"Aqila, I haven't seen any winged shadows or anything," he said while cautiously mounting Talon. "How did things go?"

"Well enough." Aqila climbed onto Talon's back.

"Where's Jai?"

"He changed his mind."

"What's up?"

"I don't know. He lied to me." She urged Talon to fly off. Their journey would take several days.

"He lied? How do you know? Wait, don't answer that. Why didn't you call him out on it?"

"The time wasn't right. It's hard to explain."

"Well, that doesn't change that the Jungle tribe requested your expertise."

"Yeah, I just have this feeling that something is off. Right now, I don't know if it is Jai, the Jungle tribe, or whoever is tailing me. I tried using the sight, but I can't now."

"Well, let's keep going forward with what we know. Besides, we can handle ourselves. Maybe it's for the best."

"I hope you're right."

*****

Jai sighed with relief once he saw Talon fly off. He wanted to tell Aqila about his father. He really did. But, for some reason, he could not bring himself to tell her. Not because he didn't trust her; he didn't want her to find him selfish. The world was crazy and in chaos, and while she was working hard to do her part, he was reconnecting with his father. He had so many questions for him. Jai believed he would better help the world if he weren't constantly fighting the feeling of abandonment, longing, and utter confusion. He trusted that closure was what he needed.

"I thought you were going with them," Arin approached him.

"Something came up," he replied, keeping his back turned toward her.

"What's wrong?"

"Nothing. Why do you ask?"

"It just feels like you are hiding something. More like you're holding something back."

He groaned at his rising conflicting feelings.

"Jai, what's going on?"

"My soul is screaming for closure. I've been pushing the feeling away for such a long time, and I can't anymore. I can't keep going on trying to be a hero, a Legend, when my mind is so void of connection. I just want my family; the one thing that I want so bad has been forever out of reach for me. I have pleaded to the Stars just to let me remember. It's frustrating. I hate feeling so empty. Now, it's like I have this slither of an opportunity to find everything I'm looking for."

"Then take it."

"What?"

"Take the opportunity. I'm not sure what this is all about, but if it's causing you this much stress, then go find everything you are looking for."

Arin touched his shoulder gently. Jai turned to face her, "Just between the two of us?"

"Only between the two of us, that's my word."

"I—I saw my father. It was almost like the Universe wanted us to bump into each other today. I want to go to visit him as soon as possible because I don't know what the future holds. Especially with Agni running amuck."

Arin stifled her gasp, "Jai! That's amazing! Why are you concerned about taking time to visit your father?"

"I don't want to be selfish. We are still in a war. Agni is looking to kill us. Calida and Beamer just died. Cahya is off on his own. Everyone is working hard to put a stop to Agni. If I go there, then I'm not here to help."

"That's not selfish, Jai. That's normal. You haven't been able to remember for such a long time. These are normal feelings. You don't have to hide them. We all care about you. We are here literally to serve you and help you. I won't tell anyone, but I don't want you to go alone. You are the Legend, and Agni has it out for you. So let me go with you."

"You know you don't have to—"

"I'm going! Just let me know when you're ready."

"I'll be ready within the hour." He watched Arin return to the cabin. Jai was relieved that she was so supportive. However, he also felt horrible for lying to Aqila. It wasn't like she would not have understood. Maybe it was for the best. She probably would have wanted to postpone her meeting with the Jungle tribe to go with him. Not telling her was for the best. Aqila was a true Windmaster. She thinks, communicates, and does. Jai's passionate drive would be met with a flurry of questions from her. Arin, on the other hand, was passionate about life and people. She was like a warm, protective ring of fire, wanting to support his ambitions.

"I'm ready," she smiled with her pretty, dimpled right cheek.

"That was fast. I said you had an hour, not ten minutes." He smirked.

"And now I'm here!"

"All right, let's walk." He led the way through the forest.□

"Not that I'm opposed to walking the entire way, but let's grab some horses from the stables in Lower Ember before we get too far on our way."

"Seems like you don't have the endurance for this journey," Jai joked.

Arin slammed her shoulder fiercely into his arm, causing him to groan. "Please, I'm from Kindle. Nothing tests your endurance more than living in a desert, not that you would understand."

"Competitive, are we?"

"Jai, all Firehearts are competitive," she whispered, "it's in our nature." The pair laughed as they left the forest and entered Lower Ember. They hurried to the stables to grab horses for their journey. "So, where are we going, exactly?"

"Upper Ember, Comet Town," Jai replied after watching Arin mount her chosen horse, a black stallion, with extreme ease. He tried to follow her motion. However, it was not as smooth and effortless. His horse was pale gray with a charcoal mane and tail.

"Well, this is going to be easy then."

"What makes you say that?" he asked as they both gave their horses a kick.

"Comet Town is for the affluent. Only twenty or so families live there. Seems like you are from a well-to-do family."

"I can't say that I know. But before we go, thanks for coming with me. It means a lot to have you here right now."

"Of course. I'm glad you trusted me."

Jai shook his head. "I'd trust you with my life."

"And I trust you with mine." The Firehearts rode in blissful silence for a long time—hours. They passed through the trodden villages of Lower Ember.

"It seems like Agni has slowed his recruiting process by the looks of things here," Arin murmured.

"Yeah, many people lost their lives in that border fight. The worst thing is that they really believe in Agni's cause."

"What is his cause? If all he wants is to take over and lead the Firehearts, how is that a cause?"

"Because it's deeper than that. He wants to kill all of the Legends. He believes that Legends like myself are the problem with the world. In his mind, Legends bring imbalance, with one person from every nation being significantly stronger than the rest. For oppressed people, that message is music to their ears. His vendetta seemed almost personal when he was about to kill me. He said something about needing to end me before I destroyed the world."

"What? Destroyed the world? What does that mean? Personal, how?"

"I don't know what that could mean. I don't know if it has something to do with my memories. I said his vendetta seemed personal because it feels like something happened to him to make him truly believe that."

"I wonder why the Universe hasn't removed his gift, though. Like the people of old."

"I don't know, Arin. Hopefully, Aqila and Boaz will find out something about the Waterbearer tribes."

"I heard that we now have a Neptune to deal with too? When will it end? What if there is a nemesis in every nation that we will eventually have to topple to achieve peace?"

"If that's the case, then we will topple every one of them and achieve peace," Jai replied confidently.

"We're here. This is Comet Town." Arin pulled the reins, causing the black stallion to halt.

"Whoa," Jai said to his horse as he took in the beautiful view. There was a gold-painted water fountain in the center of the town, and all the houses had multiple stories with ornate craftsmanship. It looked like it belonged to the DragonLord himself and not like an Emberite town.

"Like I said, you have a well-to-do father." Arin wiggled her eyebrows. "Stay on the outskirts, and I'll ask for . . ."

"Oh no, we're going in together."

"But Jai, this is risky! You don't even have a hood. We wouldn't want you to get caught in the clutches of some Agni supporter."

"I'll be fine. If something feels weird, we'll come straight back," Jai spoke firmly.

Arin sighed as she rode the lean black stallion into Comet Town while Jai followed closely behind. The difference between the two Embers was night and day. They had been divided for such a long time: a prosperous, flourishing Upper and a war-riddled, downtrodden Lower. *Was it even possible for the two to ever become one?*

"Jai! I've been calling you!"

He shook his head violently. "Sorry, I was lost in thought."

"I could tell. But where are we going exactly? I don't feel good about us going from door to door."

"Or you could stay here while I have a look around," Jai suggested.

"Absolutely not! You're not going alone. What was the point of me coming along?"

"To keep me company, like I knew you wanted to," Jai joked. When Arin started tussling his already mangled locks, he groaned. "Okay, okay! I get it you're coming with me. Let's go."

CHAPTER 16

Tiber felt like she was going to pass out. Cove watched her antics, smirking. "I can always send you back if you aren't brave enough."

"It's not funny, Cove! I almost killed her the last time. I planned on spending the rest of my life avoiding Windmasters altogether. I don't want her to see me and kill me!"

"Calm down. You don't even look the same, remember? It will be okay. Don't forget that I'm here, and Kavi, the future ruler of Kashmala, is my friend. Everything will be okay."

More like the future ruler of sending me to my immediate death! Like this Kavi is going to be thrilled to meet the person who almost killed his fiancé.

A loud squawk was heard in a secluded spot in the jungle, where the river's pace was rapid. Tiber took several deep breaths as she viewed a winged creature causing a massive shadow in the clear skies. The flaps were inaudible, but nonetheless, it was drawing closer. Tiber couldn't see a rider. She gently patted Mika's sleek, black head. She was antsy as well.

As the owl landed, Cove went to greet the riders. "Aqila, thank you for honoring my request."

Tiber's heart dropped at the raspy-sounding voice. "Of course, Cove. I wouldn't neglect my duty. My long-time friend accompanied me. Meet Boaz. Bo, this is Cove."

A Landkeeper suddenly dismounted the owl. "Nice to meet you." He extended a hand to Cove, and the pair shook hands.

"You're a strong man, Boaz."

"Thank you, likewise."

Aqila approached Tiber, who wanted to faint. Their eyes met. Aqila's eyes looked like liquid silver as they bore through Tiber's navy eyes. "You must have had a serious ordeal. I'm Aqila the Seer. What's your name?"

"Talia—my name is Talia."

"Well, Talia, why don't you tell me what happened?" Aqila sat with her legs folded, her hands gently resting on her knees.

"Go ahead," Cove urged Tiber.

She looked to Cove, who was smiling at her, then to Boaz, leaning on Aqila's owl. Tiber took a deep breath. "My tribe thinks I murdered my father. I got in trouble with one of my tribe brothers, and we had to account. The tribe brother lied, pinning the guilt on me. I was preparing for punishment when I sought out my father to tell him the truth. When I got to his tent, he had a stab wound. He said a few words to me before he died. The tribe brother who lied about me saw me at my father's side and accused me of murder. The tribe rallied at the call and chased me. I fled for my life and Mika's. One of my tribe sisters believes me, and she's been trying to prove my innocence. But now there's been another murder, this time of an elder. The brother who lied is now taking over my tribe."

Aqila immediately stood to her feet and slowly walked toward Tiber. "I'm sorry for what you are suffering.

However, when you inflict pain on others, it is bound to return upon you."

Tiber's breath hitched as Aqila came closer, towering over her. "Aqila, please."

"Hoping you would never see me again, Tiber?"

Cove immediately flung a water whip in Aqila's direction. She smirked and deoxygenated the water whip. "Aqila, stop. I asked you to come because we need help!"

"Cove, relax." Aqila stepped away from Tiber. "I knew something was suspicious when you asked for my audience. I knew she was Tiber when I laid eyes on her. Knowing you lied and she nearly killed me, I could have killed both of you without even touching down to land. That is if I had wanted to. Were you expecting Kavi, Cove? You know he would have been furious that you lied to me. One of the reasons I'm glad he was too busy to make the trip. We wouldn't want to sever alliances, would we?"

"How did you know it was me?"

"You've gone through the Changing, but your voice still has the same timbres. You also slipped up, referring to the cat as Mika. You were also insanely vague in describing your troubling experience."

"Aqila, I'm sorry for deceiving you, but we need help. A chief has been murdered, and Neptune could be involved," Cove explained.

"Neptune? I'm interested in finding any strings that lead to him. I must admit I am not thrilled at this deceptive arrangement; however, at the moment, that is not what's most important. Tiber, I need you to answer a few direct questions from me." Aqila returned to her previous sitting posture.

"All right." Tiber nodded in agreement.

"Is Nahal involved in this situation?"

"Yes, he tried to pin the problem on me."

"What problem?"

"After our battle, several of our men were injured and unconscious, and a few died from their wounds. We had been unconscious for weeks. My father wanted us to tell the tribe what happened, me and Nahal, that is."

"Who is your father?"

"My father was Chief Dalit."

"Did Nahal see you as you went to talk to your father, or did you only see him after your father was murdered?"

"After he was murdered, while I was holding him in my hands, crying for him to come back, that was when Nahal came."

"I thought the Waterbearer tribes made a decree for the tribe, something likened to a will. Did your father have one?"

"He did, but it is missing. The tribe is in the thirty-one-day period to elect a new chief."

"How much time is left?"

"Fifteen days."

"Who is the tribe sister who believed in you, and do you still have communication with her?"

"She's our tribe medic, Sita."

"Last question. Are you and Nahal still supporting Neptune?"

"Nahal is; however, I am not. I have used the Changing as a fresh start, and I believe in the Universe," Tiber replied confidently.

"Aqila, he's back," Boaz warned.

"As I thought. Talon, attack!" The Great Gray Owl immediately flew into the air. "Head back to your tribe. Someone's been tailing me."

"Tiber, go back and alert Kano. Tell him to meet me. Have Rilian usher the women and children back home," Cove ordered. Tiber hurried away, riding Mika. "I can help you out here. It is the least I can do," he called to Aqila.

Boaz, Cove, and Aqila looked up to see Talon ferociously attack another winged creature. Its rider expertly dove into the clearing. It was a man; his back was turned toward them. His long braid gently bounced in the wind. "You should let me escape if you know what's good for you."

"You're trespassing in my territory." Cove used the river to aim a water whip attack at the intruder. Employing several backflips and twists, the man avoided every attack. Cove continued to attack, and Boaz aimed a rock fury at the opponent. It was futile. The man was too nimble.

Aqila stood in shock at the realization that this man was a Windmaster. When he turned to face them, he shot a mighty blast of wind at Boaz and Cove. The blast hurled them back into two separate tree trunks, a force so robust that it rendered them both unconscious.

"It's just you and me. Let me off. We don't need to fight. I mean, you're a Seer and a Legend. You'd wipe the floor with me."

Aqila was angry. "You've been tailing me for weeks! Explain yourself, or I will attack!"

"If I could, I would, but I've been enlisted in a dangerous mission that requires a great deal of secrecy. I need you to let me go now."

Aqila honed her wind blade and whirled a mighty wind swipe at her opponent. The violent, gusty battle ensued. This man was obviously a Storm, but his martial arts proficiency was incredible. He engaged Aqila in a whizzing hand-to-hand fight. Aqila was fast and elusive, but he had a sheer strength behind his attacks that she could not match. Her only edge was to try and outmaneuver him. She was outmatched in fighting technical ability, but she was leaner and quicker. Aqila knew she could probably use an advanced technique on him, but that was not the Windmaster way.

"Enough!" The man blasted her backward. "I must report back. My name is Haneul." He hurried to his dasher, a red-tailed hawk. "I took an oath, Aqila. I'm on your side," he whispered before flying off. Talon began to follow suit.

"Talon, land." The owl hooted ferociously in disagreement, huffing in anger. Aqila tilted her head in authority, and the owl obeyed his rider. Aqila hurried to Cove and Boaz. She heard rustling in the jungle. Tiber had returned with a muscular Jungle tribesman. "Let's get them back to the tribe," she ordered Tiber, pointing to the unconscious men.

Tiber looked concerned and spoke to Kano, "It's okay. Aqila is a friend of the tribe. We came a little too late to help."

Kano laid Cove on Mika's back and placed Boaz on Talon. As they entered the tribe hub, everyone's eyes were on Aqila. She was taller than almost everyone in the tribe. Her gray hair and silver eyes are an anomaly among the Waterbearers. "Aqila, let's go. Kano will get us when they wake up," Tiber called as she climbed into the tree tent. Aqila observed her path and launched herself to the top. Tiber led her to the tent she shared with Rilian.

"I thank you."

"It's me who should be thanking you," Tiber replied.

"You live with someone?"

"Yeah, a vanguard, her name is Rilian. Everyone has been really kind to me since I've been here." Tiber looked at Aqila, who had to duck at every turn. The tent was not made for such tall people.

"I'm sorry about your father, Tiber. I can account on your behalf, but it will not work if Nahal takes control of the tribe. He will negate any progress you make. We don't have a lot of time. This is what we need to do. We need to pit Neptune against Nahal. We also need to find your father's decree so the tribe can name the new chief. I can explain what happened to a new chief, which will set you free. Tell me about this other murder."

"An elder Moonsayer was murdered. Chelan said that Sita told him that it was not a natural death. She's the medic, so she would know. She got hair and skin samples and a piece of her tongue because it was blue." Tiber curled her lip close to her nose, remembering what Chelan told her.

"Are you sure he said blue?"

"Positive."

"It was the same poison you used on me. It was used on Jai as well."

"What? Is he okay?"

"Yes, he's okay now, Tiber. Where did you get yours from?"

"Well, Nahal said he got it from the Beach tribe. But I had to go to Theyra to get my dose. Everyone in my tribe has to get their vial from Theyra, except Nahal. He is one of Neptune's most loyal followers, and he really believes that Neptune will save the tribe. In exchange for Nahal's unwavering loyalty, Nahal gets special favors," Tiber replied.

"Theyra, is that so? Things are really getting interesting," Aqila murmured.

What business does Neptune have in Theyra? Also, who in Theyra would have ties to Neptune? The Landkeepers are in a civil war. Who has time for Neptune? Unless, of course, Neptune is aiding one side over the other. At this rate, all nations will be involved with this Agni-Neptune debacle.

"Tiber, Cove is awake and on his way," Kano returned. "And Aqila, Boaz is asking for you." As Kano exited, Aqila dashed out of the tent at the speed of light. Tiber smiled. Who would have ever thought that a Windmaster and a Landkeeper could be such good friends? Several moments passed, and Cove entered the tent, rubbing the back of his head.

"What happened?" Tiber hurried to his side.

"I got knocked out. That's the short version."

"Who was tailing Aqila?"

"Don't know, whoever it was, they were so nimble. I think it was a Windmaster. A huge blast of wind knocked me back, and I hit my head on a tree trunk. Are you okay? How are things between you and Aqila?"

"We're over the past and are going forward. You were right about having information of interest to her. She seems really interested in Neptune. She thinks it was a poison that killed Elder Akay, the same poison I used on her. Aqila even said that it was used on Jai, the Fireheart Legend."

"We must get more information from Sita and Chelan at the summer festival."

"My thoughts exactly."

Aqila returned with Boaz. "But you're going to have to be careful. Tiber's tribe is still looking for her and could seize her at the festival if you're not careful."

"She's going with me, so she'll be safe," Cove said, brushing off Aqila's warning.

"I'm serious, Cove. You don't even know half of it. The last time a leader ignored my warning, they wished they hadn't. Nahal is willing to go to extremes to silence Tiber, so it is safe to assume that Neptune is as well. Neptune has a powerful ally in Agni. Agni, who wants to kill all of the Legends!"

"That's Agni's motivation? Then what is Neptune after?" Cove asked.

"That's what I'm trying to find out. Something is linking them together. If this keeps up, all of the nations are going to be swept up in this chaos. Just be careful, okay? If I have any insights pertaining to this, I'll reach out. Boaz, are you ready?"

"Yeah, let's go. It was a pleasure to meet you, Cove and Tiber." The Landkeeper and Windmaster left the tent and hurried to Talon. They flew up over the Jungle tribe, taking in the breathtakingly lush views.

"Who was that man, Aqila? He was so strong; I mean, was he a part of the WindGuard?"

"No, he wasn't. I don't know who he is or what he wants. All I know is that he wasn't trying to hurt me. He actually kept asking me to let him off."

"What? You are a powerful Windmaster—"

"No, he could have hurt me if he wanted to. He was stronger than me, and his fighting techniques were more advanced than mine. I had to evade and use my smaller frame to outmaneuver him. We ended in a stalemate because he stopped the fight."

"Okay, you definitely need to talk to Kavi about this," Boaz exclaimed.

"I know, and I will. Bo, have you seen Waterbearers in Theyra?"

"No, why?"

"Because Neptune is sending Waterbearers to Theyra to pick up vials of that paralyzing poison. Tiber told me about it. I don't know why I didn't think about it before. I was in Theyra when I was poisoned. I can't believe that I overlooked that fact. Maybe Neptune is supporting one side of the war or something."

"It's possible. Aqila, I need you to drop me off at the Theyra-Ember border, and I need to go home."

"Do you know something?"

"No, and that's the problem! I must stop this war. If it doesn't stop, we will never slow Neptune down. If we can slow Neptune down, that will leave Agni vulnerable."

"Boaz, how do you plan to stop a war that has been going on for several years?"

"Do you trust me?"

"Of course, but I don't want you to die due to the lack of a good plan!"

"Hear me out. Let me at least get both sides to agree to a ceasefire. Then I'll tell you everything. Until then, I must do this on my own."

"What's the point of friendship if I'm just going to let you go off on this death mission alone?"

"You're not letting me go off on a death mission alone. You're letting me fulfill my purpose—chase my special destiny. Jai, Tora, Sheraga, the Flamethrowers, and Cahya are all fighting for the sake of their people. Tiber is fighting for her tribe. And you, Aqila, are trying to help the other nations while keeping your people from being dragged into a complete mess. As much as I want to help you, Jai, and Tiber, I must help my people first. As a Landkeeper, I owe them that. Just drop me off at the border. That'll be fine."

"I can do better. I'll drop you off at home. And if you need anything, I'll be there."

"Thanks, Aqila. You know, sometimes I wonder if Ila and Basir had a friendship like ours."

"We may never know for sure, but I think ours is better because I know that we won't allow anyone to burn the bridge between us."

"No, we won't. Do you think you can help Tiber before the end of the thirty-one days?"

"I have a plan to catch Nahal, regardless of finding out Neptune's identity. I need to tie up a few loose ends, and I know the perfect person to help me with that."

"Do you think that man will tail you again?"

"I'm not sure, but I know his signature now."

"His signature? What's that?"

"Red feathers, his dasher sheds its feathers a lot. He's dyed them red. I don't know what that symbolizes. Either way, he wasn't trying to harm me. Until I know anything else, it would be better to leave him be."

"Be careful while I'm gone, Aqila."

"I will. And don't get yourself into too much trouble. Be careful not to fan the flames of either side unless there is a clear right or wrong."

"Of course, Storm, of course."

CHAPTER 17

Sita was delicately placing a spoonful of fish chowder in her mouth. The warm, savory dish relaxed her completely. Shasa was to her right, and Nahal was to her left. The evening was so peaceful. All of her problems were becoming a distant memory. Usually, the women would serve the men, but with Shasa expecting, Mahak insisted on serving everyone. He always seemed so strict; it was nice to see him laid back for once. Muraco, Shasa, and Mahak were reminiscing about old times. And Nahal was pleasant company.

"What do you think of the soup?" she asked Nahal.

"It's absolute bliss! I love it," Nahal replied.

Sita laughed at the droplets of food sliding from his mouth as he answered. Nahal shielded his face in embarrassment. Sita took her cloth napkin and gently wiped his mouth.

Mahak cleared his throat. "I have an announcement."

Surprised, Sita glanced at Shasa, who was beaming with excitement.

"The Tribe of Snow and Ice have endured much. All of our strength comes from our family unit. We see each other as brothers and sisters—an extension of family. Loving marriages are the foundation on which our culture stands. So, with great honor, I'd like to extend a proposal to our wonderful Sita on behalf of my son, Nahal."

Sita, choking on her soup, began coughing frantically. Shasa patted her back. Nahal offered her water. She gulped the water down, relieving her airways. She took a deep breath.

"Are you okay?" Nahal whispered.

"Yes, I'm just taken by surprise."

"It would be a good match," Muraco chimed in.

Mahak's eyes widened with concern. "Forgive me for surprising you. I'm glad you're all right. Sita, you and Nahal were selected by Chief Dalit as a suitable match prior to his unfortunate death. I am just the messenger. Of course, this marriage would not be allowed to produce any children. My oldest has a child on the way, and Sita is a medic. Why don't you two take some time to talk about the arrangement?"

"Thank you, Father. Sita, let's take a walk." Nahal extended his hand, to which Sita graciously accepted. The pair went outside and walked through the tribe. An awkward silence plagued them.

"Sita, I didn't know anything about this. I promise I didn't."

"What do you think of the arrangement?"

"What I think is not important. As the woman in the arrangement, it is more important for me to know how you feel about things," Nahal replied.

"And as the woman, I ask again, what do you think?"

"I'm happy. I agree with the late chief that you and I are a suitable match."

"A childless match."

"For that, I'm glad! I don't know how the rest of them do it, but I can't imagine falling in love and making a life with someone to watch them die."

"It's not like there's another choice."

"I'm working on another way. I'll do whatever it takes—"

"You say that a lot."

"Because I mean it! Aren't you tired of this? This struggling tribe? Our sister tribes are flourishing; why can't we? Why can't we get rid of this curse? If there is any chance that we can end the curse, I'll take it. I'll do *whatever it takes* to help this tribe thrive, even if it makes me the villain. I'm fighting so that fifty years from now, our people can have a better life."

"I know about Neptune, Nahal. I don't feel it's safe. I don't want to sway you. I want us to be able to talk about things."

"Neptune is a complicated situation, but he is the only one unsatisfied with this hell that we are in. So much so that he's trying to fix things, I believe that with everything that I am. I know you may not want me as a husband—"

"Not at all! Nahal, maybe you're so busy with Neptune that you can't see that most of the women in this tribe would be honored to be your wife."

"I'm not concerned with that—with what others think. I'm only concerned with what you think of me. Could you see a future with me?"

"I have a lot on my mind. This is so sudden, and I'm just confused right now. It's not that I have doubts about your ability to be a great husband, but I need more time."

"We just learned of this tonight. I understand that you need more time. I respect that; really, I do."

A light flurry of snow began to fall as the pair stood several feet apart. Sita had been looking at the mink boots on her feet, shuffling them in the snow. She wished that she didn't know about Neptune. She wished that she wasn't involved with Tiber's situation. Then this would be such an easy yes. "So what now," she whispered.

"If you'd allow me, I'd like to walk you home."

She nodded, slowly meeting his gaze. However, this time, it was Nahal who looked away. The pair walked back in silence. Upon reaching her tent, Sita turned to Nahal. "Thank you."

Gently brushing tiny flecks of snow from her hair, Nahal smiled. "Good night, Sita."

He waited for her to enter her tent before slowly turning away to leave. Sita pulled the door flap back, taking one last glance as he walked away.

What do I do? She prepared to retire for the evening. She set her curly hair free. Her knees weak, she fell to the floor and cried. It was a pain that had been wearing on her for a long time. Through everything that had been going on, she'd tried to stay strong. But she could no longer keep her facade in the confines of her own abode. She wished her father was there. She hugged her knees. Never had she felt more alone. Stings of envy washed over her as she thought about Tiber and Nahal. They were lucky to have a sibling. She wished that she had a brother or sister to talk to and put her heart at ease.

"Sita?"

"Come in, Shasa," Sita answered, quickly wiping her eyes.

"My sweet girl!" Shasa slowly walked in to sit beside her. "It pains me that these beautiful steel-blue eyes are no longer dancing with happiness. I know that arranged marriages can be shocking, but the chief takes a lot of time to pair a suitable match. I know I've been a bit upset with Nahal about how things have been handled with Tiber. But in all truth, Nahal cares a lot about this tribe. He's intelligent and strong and—"

"I know. He's a bright spot in the tribe. Yet, his demons are like the dark side of the moon. That's what I don't like. I wish he'd put his demons in the light so he can heal and get help." Seeing that, Shasa's eyes widened. Sita stopped, clearing her throat. "Forgive me. I'm just tired. Much has been happening. I understand that Chief Dalit put much time into matches for the sake of the tribe. It would be an honor to marry Nahal."

Shasa smiled with happiness. "That is wonderful news. Sita, we all have areas to improve. But that's such a wonderful part of marriage; we help each other become better. And since Muraco and I will be having a child, you and Nahal will be able to enjoy a long life together. You are very fortunate."

The weight of Shasa's words crashed into Sita's heart. These were Shasa's last few months. The child she's carrying will inevitably be the end of her. Sita felt guilty for complaining.

"I am very fortunate. Thank you, Shasa. Please extend thanks to your family. I will accept the proposal. I will tell Nahal myself tomorrow."

Sita stood and helped Shasa up. Cradling her bump, she spoke, "I'm so happy for you two. I will head home now. Please, Sita, don't worry about me. This is my destiny. This must be my path for our tribe to have a future. It's a worthy sacrifice. You get some rest now. You will be busy with wedding plans soon."

As Shasa left her tent, Sita finally understood Nahal's words. *Aren't you tired of this? This struggling tribe? Our sister tribes are flourishing; why can't we? Why can't we get rid of this curse? If there is any chance that we can end the curse, I'll take it. I'll do whatever it takes to help this tribe thrive, even if it makes me the villain. I'm fighting so that fifty years from now, our people can have a better life.*

But she realized that Nahal's judgment was clouded. "Neptune is just playing us, using our situation to his advantage," she mumbled to herself.

Stepping outside, the snow was picking up. She looked up to the moon.

Such a beautiful sky. Such a beautiful moon. What have we done that we must pay with blood? I'm a medic. My people are dying, and I can't save them. I want it to stop. My heart is just so heavy that it hurts. I'm tired of people dying. I'm willing to give up everything and start again if it would save lives. Oh, beautiful moon, can you not see that we are desperate? Is there something we are doing wrong? If so, give us a sign so we can fix it! Let our tribe be restored to our former greatness, please. Let us have our equality back so we all can be free to marry and start families like in the days of old. I'm the only medic. I can't have children because of this curse! What have I done? I have led a life of service; please spare us. Moon, can't you see! I want to marry Nahal. But I fear he will self-destruct because of this curse. He will do anything to free this tribe. So please help him—help us. There's nothing left to believe in . . . please.

CHAPTER 18

The Jungle tribe's atmosphere was bustling with activity. The women were excited about preparing for the summer festival. Anahita managed the women in the dress tent as they clamored with excitement. Tiber felt like she was going to be sick.

"Ladies, I don't think this shade will do," Anahita called out as she gently turned Tiber around, looking at her indigo dress.

"What's wrong with this one?" Tiber groaned. She had been held captive in the tent for two hours.

"Baby, this color is doing absolutely nothing for your eyes," Anahita whispered. "Misu, bring me another, please."

A teenage girl brought Anahita another dress. When Tiber saw the color, she could only think about Nahal's eyes. "Not this one. I absolutely hate that color."

Anahita shifted uncomfortably. "Okay, that's fine . . . Misu, let's go a bit more basic."

"Can I come back tomorrow?" Tiber asked.

"Of course. I have no objection to that." Anahita clasped her hands. "Misu, I need to do some alterations. Could you put the other dresses away?"

"Yes, Anahita!"

Tiber left the tent only to see Rilian smirking at her. "What?"

"You look exhausted. From what I've heard, you were being difficult."

"Rilian, I was in there for hours." Tiber groaned.

"Well, you have tomorrow. Let's go home." The pair went to their tent. Tiber followed Rilian inside, and the quick, heavy steps of the cats were not far behind. "So, you never told me who you're going with . . . or are you just going to mingle?"

"Um—uh, since I'm going to meet my tribesmen, Cove thought we should go together so to not draw suspicion."

"That's nice. That will be good for him. He never goes anywhere. I mean, I understand. Running a tribe takes a lot of work. But he's still a young man, so it is great that he will get a chance to enjoy the day. You may even see my mother."

"Your mother?"

"Yeah, Chief Marina," Rilian said as if it wasn't a big deal. "Don't look so shocked. How did you think Rio and I got these ocean-blue eyes?"

"How come you're here and not there?"

"Eh, our father was from this tribe. After he passed, Rio and I came here. We feel close to him this way. We keep in touch with our mother and older brother, Triton."

"So, are you going to visit your mother? Or are you mingling?"

"Kano and his father are coming to meet my family. This year's festival will be a special one for our family. Triton and his wife just had a baby. It will be our first time seeing him, for me and Rio, that is."

"Congrats! I'm so happy for your family!" Tiber smiled at her friend. She was hopeful that Sita and Chelan would have some more information so they could update Aqila. The Windmaster was already working on a plan. The day was getting late, and Rilian had left the tent. Tiber began preparing food for the evening.

"Permission to enter."

"Come in, Cove," Tiber replied.

"Are you ready for the festival?"

"Not really. I need to go back to the dress tent in order to have something to wear."

"I've taken care of that. Misu will be dropping it off tomorrow. So that's taken care of. I'm actually excited. I never have the opportunity to go out and have fun with people my age, and I can't wait. I hope your friends were able to get some more information. Either way, I've had Kano and Rio do some side investigating work."

"And? Have they found anything out?"

"Have they? Listen to this. Neptune has a following in every nation except the Firehearts. He even has a small following in Wyndhm but nothing in Kashmala."

"Wait! What if the man that was tailing Aqila was part of Neptune's following?"

"I was thinking about that. Aqila and Kavi are definitely going to want to know about this."

"Aqila was afraid this would happen." Tiber sighed. "Who would have thought that what we do now will impact the world, every nation, and every person."

"I know. That's why this festival is of great importance. We can't stand out. We've got to have fun and kick back with everyone else. If we don't, we risk getting discovered."

Tiber agreed. They could not risk getting discovered. A lot was riding on the transfer of information at this one event. She hoped that all was well for Sita and Chelan. Everyone just had to hang in there for one more day. If her father were alive, he would have accompanied her to the summer festival. He would have introduced her to suitors and made some recommendations for her. Her sister used to tell her stories of her first summer festival. It was nostalgic and made Tiber miss Shasa deeply.

*****

Chelan's eyes widened in disbelief. "So, you're okay with all of this?"

Sita was growing increasingly annoyed at having to repeat herself, "Yes, I am!"

"What are you thinking? What about Tiber? She is counting on you to come to the festival—and without the man who blames her for killing her father!"

"Don't you think I know that? I'm working on it. I have to talk to Nahal, and we will be attending the festival."

"And how are you going to meet Tiber if you are with him?"

"I said I'm working on it!"

"Well, you have to figure something out fast. The festival is right on our heels."

"I'm aware. I just have to convince Nahal that this Neptune thing is wrong! If I could do that, then Tiber could clear her name, and maybe we could find this master manipulator and get rid of him for good."

"That's a lot of ifs. I want to help, but I am baffled as to what's going on right now." He sat beside her. "I thought that we had evidence to pin Nahal to a crime. I thought we were helping Tiber. That's why I was caught off guard to learn that you are actually considering his proposal."

"That's the thing! There has been no evidence that Nahal had anything to do with Chief Dalit or Elder Akay's murders. If anything, Nahal is obsessed with making the tribe better. So we are back at square one. We don't know anything. And I don't think it's a good idea for Tiber to return until we know who did this."

"Okay, so Nahal is off the hook . . . for now. So, who did it?"

"There's only one answer that makes sense; Neptune had to have done it."

"We would have noticed an outsider."

Sita's mouth dropped. "That's right! Neptune . . . is one of us. How did I not put it together? Nahal is rarely gone unless he is given an assignment by Chief Dalit. This Neptune knows enough about the Moon Curse to convince our warriors, Nahal, and Tiber that he could end the curse. Even our sister tribes don't know the intricacies of the Moon Curse. I don't know why it feels like I'm missing something."

"But why the chief and why Elder Akay?" Chelan asked.

"I don't know. I haven't heard of Neptune other than some rumors that he wanted to make the Waterbearer tribes one united tribe. After that fell apart, I hadn't heard of him other than what Tiber told me. However, the only reason to get Elder Akay out of the way would be to leave our tribe without a Moonsayer."

"Well, go find Nahal! Convince him to go to the festival. I'll come too. Once I find Tiber, I'll distract Nahal so that you can speak to her. If that doesn't work, I'll tell her all of this."

"You're going to have to tell her. If I go with Nahal, it will be hard to separate us, especially since we will be betrothed by then."

Sita left Chelan to work on herbal teas and made her way to Nahal's tent. "Nahal?"

Nahal was outside within minutes. Happiness danced in his cerulean eyes. "Good morning."

"Good morning. I just wanted to apologize for last night. You were trying to be considerate of me—"

"There's nothing to apologize for. It was a surprise for both of us. I'm about to make my rounds and see what's needed. Do you need anything from me?"

"I accept the proposal. I do feel like we need to improve our communication. I feel like you are keeping me in the dark about some things. I know you are going to be busy, but maybe we could spend some time together at the festival?"

"Ah, the summer festival is approaching in a couple of days. I honestly did not plan to attend; much of the tribe is going, and our numbers are already pitifully small. Hmm, do you really want to go?"

"With you, yes."

"Then I'll make it happen."

"Thank you."

"Of course, now I really do need to make my rounds. Maybe we can have dinner with the family again?"

"I'll be there."

Sita was relieved. As she returned to her lair, Chelan told her about meeting Tiber the day prior. She had gone through the Changing. Sita felt horrible that Tiber experienced that alone. The Changing was an excruciating process of undergoing puberty in one night. It was physically painful and mentally exhausting. It usually happens between the ages of seventeen to nineteen. Until a woman experiences the Change, she looks like a child in face and body. Sita remembered her own Changing. Her father held her hand the entire time. Elder Akay made tea and salves to try to ease the pain. Her clothes had ripped off her body. He wrapped her in blankets until he returned with her new wardrobe. Would she recognize Tiber when she goes to the festival? Either way, Chelan has already seen her, so he'd recognize her. Sita wondered what her new appearance would be like. She also wondered how Tiber would take the news of her and Nahal's betrothal and the revelation that Neptune was a member of their tribe.

CHAPTER 19

Two days passed, and the morning of the summer festival was beautiful. The cloudless sky was the clearest shade of baby blue. The Beach tribe was packed with people. Tiber couldn't afford to lose sight of Cove, or she would be lost. He would brush his shoulder with hers now and then, letting her know he was still there.

"Marina is going to announce the beginning of the festival, so we must stand by the ocean until she does. We can't mingle with any other tribe until she starts the festival," Cove instructed. He and Tiber made their way to the sandy ocean shore and took a spot near other Jungle tribe members.

Looking around, she noticed that the Tribe of Snow and Ice was not represented. A feeling of dread began to consume her. Rilian, who wasn't too far away from her, gave her a nudge. "The Snow tribe is always late. However, they have the greatest distance to travel. They'll come. Don't worry. Besides, you look too pretty not to smile."

Tiber smiled at her friend. She was right. Cove had Misu deliver a breathtakingly beautiful royal blue dress with sheer sleeves. It fell right past her calves and had silver beading along the boat neckline. She really liked it. Rilian looked absolutely radiant as well in her long ombre blue dress. It had cap sleeves and a front slit that came below her knee. Rilian had several bangles in various shades of blue to match her dress. While she was distracted, she heard the beating drums. Her tribe had arrived. Nervousness and excitement traveled through her veins. Cove squeezed her hand.

"You're from the Jungle tribe. You don't know them, remember?" he whispered, tickling her ear with his breath.

"You're right," Tiber admitted. She could not blow her cover. As her tribe arrived, Tiber noticed how many people came. Her tribe was the smallest of the three Waterbearer domains, but they sent the most people.

"Great stars! It's like they sent everyone they could find. Why so many of them?" Cove asked.

"If we don't secure mates from the other tribes, we'll cease to exist because of the curse. It is like a steady production. Some couples marry and have children, while others are forbidden to have children. If every family produced a child, we would have no women in our tribe. This festival is necessary for survival," Tiber explained.

"I never knew it was that critical. There goes Marina."

Tiber's jaw dropped when she set her eyes on Marina. She was pretty and looked as if she hadn't aged past twenty-five, which was impossible, seeing that Rilian and Rio, her youngest children, were in their early twenties. Her ocean-blue eyes danced like her daughter's. Rilian, Rio, and Marina strongly favored each other.

"What's her secret?" she whispered to Rilian.

"Mother swears by sea salt body scrubs and seaweed facials. But I think it's because she drinks plenty of water." Rilian giggled.

Marina's eyes scoured the Jungle tribe until they landed on her children. She smiled slightly at them.

"Good morning, Waterbearers of all tribes! We have gathered together in peace for our yearly summer festival!

This is more than just a ritual or a display of friendship. This is an event of unity, brotherhood, and happiness. In the beginning, three women were born from a small river. The oldest sister was the strongest. She could move large bodies of water at will. Neither heat nor cold could deter her. The second sister was fearless and resourceful. She could find water in other living things. She could harness that power whenever she saw fit. And the youngest sister was very spiritual. She could transform water into ice with faultless precision.

"After the stars made their revelation, the sisters could not agree on where to live, having outgrown the river. Unable to agree, the sisters made their mark where it was best for each of them. The oldest sister settled by the ocean. The second sister settled deep within the jungle. And the youngest sister traveled off the mainland to an island of snow and ice. Once a year, they would meet and reconnect with each other, keeping their sisterly bond alive.

"This festival reminds us that we are all one. Regardless of where you find it, water is water, and that will never change. We are extensions of one people—one family. The Stars ordained that we find companions among ourselves. My people, feel free to express yourselves and mingle, for we are all bearers of water." Clapping was heard immediately following Marina's words. Rilian, Kano, and Rio left Cove and Tiber alone as all the tribes began to mingle.

"We have to make this look natural. So let's enjoy some festivities as we make our way over."

Tiber knew Cove was right. They would look suspicious running over to her tribe; they had to relax and enjoy the event.

"So, was there something that you wanted to do?" As soon as the question left her lips, a sea of women flooded over to them, separating them. Tiber was pushed and shoved far away from Cove within minutes. Beach tribe girls, Snow tribe girls, Jungle tribe girls, all of them vying for the attention of the young chief. Tiber lowered her head and went her own way. She didn't want to see anymore.

Maybe if her father were alive, she might have been one of those girls, flocking to his side, fighting to be considered as suitable wife material. But that wasn't the case. Cove was a chief, and Tiber was an outlaw of our own tribe charged with murder. This lovely dress and relaxing atmosphere quickly made her forget her new reality. She was a nobody, and she had absolutely nothing. Everything around her was borrowed, including time. A deep sadness was making a home in her heart. She just wanted to give up, ball up, and cry. She should turn herself in and let Nahal have his way. He was winning anyway.

A low growl pulled her from her thoughts as Mika licked her hand several times, attempting to cheer her spirits. Tiber made her way to the rocky cliffs near the beachfront. She sat down with no regard for her new dress and no respect for her life, which was still in danger. She just sighed.

"This is not a day to spend alone." Tiber looked and saw Marina approach her.

"Good morning, Chiefess. I was just having a moment to myself."

"The number one rule of the summer festival is to leave no one isolated, for no one is an island." She peered down to the beachfront and observed Cove being swallowed by women.

"I don't blame; a young chief is quite a rarity. I know the sisters are all excited to get to know him. He usually doesn't attend the festival."

"So I've heard. Why are you up here? I mean, you're the Chiefess . . . I'm no one special."

"My sweet girl, we are all special!"

Tiber sighed as she watched the gentle waves wash upon the rocks.

"Have you ever heard the story of the dancing flamingos?"

"The dancing flamingos?" Tiber was perplexed.□

"I guess you haven't heard of it. I'm not the best storyteller, but here it goes. A flamingo couple hatched a young girl chick along the banks of the great river. They raised her with love and care. They taught her everything: what to eat, when to eat, how to fly—everything. When the flamingo turned two, her mother was hunted and killed. This left her and her father.

"Her father did his best to meet his daughter's needs. This went on for years. When she was old enough to survive on her own, she was preparing to meet at the riverbanks with the other young flamingos around her age. When they were all present, an atmosphere began to overtake them, and they all started to dance. Hundreds of flamingos began dancing and dancing, and every few minutes, a male and female would take to the skies together, signifying their union.

"After the first day, the daughter went to her father and sobbed. She told him that none of the males wished to take to the skies with her. She questioned herself and compared herself to the other flamingoes. Was her neck long enough? Curved enough? Were her feathers preened enough? Was her pink plumage pink enough? Her father told her to go back and keep dancing. The daughter went back and danced again. She did this for three days. On the third day, there were hardly any males left, but when she found a mate willing to fly to the sky with her, she found a mate for life.

"The point is that regardless of what we have endured, there's someone special for everyone. We all have life trials, but that should not hinder happiness. The dance is a compatibility test. Instead of wasting time doubting your worth, keep going, dancing, expressing, and changing until you find that one. The one who wants to dance with you forever."

"Kind of reminds me of this festival," Tiber replied. "I guess I'm like that flamingo, wishing she was more."

"And the more she danced, the more she realized that she was becoming everything she wanted to be. Keep dancing. Your father would have wanted that."

Father? How did she—

Tiber violently shook her head and turned to her. Marina placed a finger upon her lips, signaling Tiber to hush. "You have eyes like your mother. We were good friends. She was in awe of your father. She, like you, ran when she saw other women flock to him. She would sit up here and sigh over and over again. I told her, 'If you don't go and start talking to him, I will put you in a net and toss you in that ocean!' Your father was sad over the loss of his first wife and was struggling with being a single parent. Every festival, they started growing closer and closer until they got married. She was a wonderful friend to me."

"Please don't tell anyone that I'm here."

"I heard what happened. And I know that you would never kill your father. Yas came looking for you. But you weren't here, obviously."

"Why are you even talking to me? Don't you want to side with Neptune?"

"Of course not. I am a believer in the Universe. I often appear neutral because I'd rather not fan flames. Tiber, listen to me. Our time may be short. Your father felt his demise coming. He entrusted me with a great secret. It's a riddle of some sort. He believed that you would understand. Listen to these words carefully, 'The world changed when the sun and moon rose together. Blood turned to ice and flames. The sun's rays burn with hate. The sea has one set of eyes but two faces. You are the new moon, and you will rise. The cat holds the key. Look in her eyes.'"

Tiber jumped to her feet. Part of the message was confusing, but she knew exactly what the other part meant. "Thank you, Marina! Grace the Universe. This was exactly what I needed." She hugged her tightly.

Marina pushed her away. "My duty here is done. Go and mingle. I fear Neptune may appear. I will do what I can to support you, but I must protect my tribe. Be careful." Marina hurried off, and Tiber rushed to the beachfront. She decided to find Chelan and Sita on her own. Cove was too busy with his audience anyway. Mika stayed by her side the entire time. She ran on the beachfront and saw the ocean waterworks show. She stopped to observe the beautiful performance. Beach dancers were standing in the ocean, manipulating the water in sync with the beating drums. As she was watching the show, she felt someone nudge her. When she looked from the corner of her eye, she saw Chelan smiling at her.

"I'm glad to see you," Tiber whispered.

"I have much to tell you regarding Nahal and Neptune."

"Good, and I have the decree. Let's go to one of those tent shops and act like we are making a trade. Meet me at that jewelry tent after this water show. We must remain discreet."

"Yes, we do. Nahal is here with Sita."

"What?"

"Don't worry, Tiber, I'll meet you later," Chelan said before walking to get a different view of the water show.

Hands firmly grasped her shoulders. "Talia, why did you run off?" It was Cove. Tiber was relieved as he looked genuinely concerned.

"I'm fine. Besides, I wouldn't want you to miss out. Like you said, you never have time for events like this."

"What are you talking about? Miss out on what?"

Tiber ignored him and continued watching the waterworks. She could sense Cove's rising frustration. She didn't want to anger him, especially after all he'd done to help her. But she was being honest. This, whatever it was, was not meant to be. She had to focus on why she was here. Her father charged her with saving her tribe, and the Universe gave her a second chance to change her destiny. Cove was an amazing person. He was kind, loyal, and strong. Tiber knew in her heart the moment he was engulfed in the crowd of Waterbearer women that, regardless, they were not meant to be. She didn't want to blur the lines of true love and fellowship. They didn't know each other that well in all honesty, so she decided it would be unwise to let her emotions misguide her.

As the waterworks ended, Cove brushed her shoulder. "I'm sorry about earlier. I had no idea that would happen, and I feel horrible about it. I—I wish you would let me make it up to you."

"There's nothing to make up. Let's go to the jewelry tent."

"Talia," Cove hurried to catch up, "what's wrong? What happened?"

"I just talked to the Chiefess for a few moments. We need to get something to trade at the jewelry shop. Please trust me." She felt Cove firmly grab her arm.

"All right, let's go," Cove murmured. Upon entering the packed jewelry tent, Cove held Tiber's hand. "I'd rather we not get separated like that again."

Tiber saw Chelan, and she dragged Cove with her to talk to him.

"I have a tribal artifact that you may like." She reached into Mika's bag and retrieved a small jewelry box with a bypass closure for cabochon stones.

"Thank you. I must say, you have a lovely acquaintance," Chelan said to Cove. In a hushed voice, he continued, "We should grab something to eat and enjoy it close to the jungle border. That puts us about a mile or so out from here. Nahal is headed this way with Sita."

Cove nodded and shook hands with Chelan. "Sounds good, do you think he is onto anything?"

Chelan shook his head. "He's distracted."

That's why he's with Sita!

Tiber felt relieved that Nahal was occupied. She handed Chelan the jewelry box. She and Cove watched Chelan head off.

"Is there something you want for lunch?" Cove asked.

"No, not really. Is there something you'd recommend?"

"Well, I guess the one thing that's hard to get unless you're from around here is a fried fish sandwich."

Tiber laughed. "Well, you've got a point there. Let's eat! I'm hungry." They quickly found some tables and asked for two fish "sandies," as they are called in the Beach tribe.

As they sat across from each other, Tiber kept looking away every time Cove made eye contact. "Could you please stop that? It's killing me!"

"I'm sorry. I feel bad that you're stuck here with me, of all people. I want you to have a good time and mingle. You work so hard, and I want you to enjoy the festival with whoever you want to spend time with."

"Are you crazy? That's what I'm trying to do! I told you that I wanted to spend the day with you. I told you when we first talked about going to the festival together. I know what happened earlier was uncalled for, but this is what I really want."

"Why? Why me?"

"Why not you? You came to me asking for help, but I've been learning so much about what tribe and family mean from you. You are the most loyal woman I have ever met under the most stressful situation. It makes me see the things I have taken for granted. I was raised to believe in the

Universe. You weren't. It's like watching a metamorphosis, with each stage more beautiful than the previous one. I feel honored to have met you at the caterpillar stage. You're in the cocoon now. I can't wait to see what's next."

"I don't know what the future holds. Regardless, I hope you accept my friendship and genuine care for the Jungle tribe's interests," Tiber responded.

"I appreciate that, Tiber. Thank you. Now, can you fill me in about what happened with the Chiefess?"

As Tiber was about to speak, Chelan arrived at their table.

"I thought we were meeting in an hour," Tiber asked.

"Bad news. The crowd near the Jungle tribe territory is thinning out. I think there's another performance happening on the beachfront. What's worse is that Nahal is there near the Jungle tribe," Chelan informed them.

"Why is Sita with Nahal?"

"Tiber, Nahal and Sita are betrothed. That's what was going on at the dinner she went to. We investigated Nahal, and he is not connected to any murder. But we realized that Neptune is from our tribe."

Tiber's eyes widened. "What! If he's in the tribe, what if he's there to harm my sister since I failed that last mission?"

Chelan shook his head. "We don't know. The only one who knows about Neptune is Nahal. That's why Sita is trying to learn what she can from him. Tiber, Neptune could be here right now. We don't know who he is."

Tiber trembled. Cove grasped her shoulders. "Nothing will happen to you while I'm around, I promise."

"We have your back, Tiber! Now, what's the jewelry box for?" Chelan asked.

"If you open it, the decree should be in there. Guard it with your life. Give it to Shasa and tell her I'm alive and well," Tiber explained.

"The decree . . . you had it?"

Lowering her head, Tiber replied, "I didn't know until a few moments ago."

Chelan sighed, "I'll guard it with my life." He stood, nodding his respect to Tiber and Cove before walking into the crowd.

Cove furrowed his brows slightly, "Where did you find the decree?"

"My father hid it in Mika's travel bag. With everything that happened, I forgot that he told me to guard Mika with my life. Mika had the decree. He said he knew everything." Tiber sobbed.

"Hey, hey, it's okay," Cove tried to comfort her.

"I can't imagine how he felt. He must have known that Neptune was in our tribe."

"You know what that also means?"

Tiber shook her head no.

"That means that even after everything that happened with Nahal and capturing Aqila, your father trusted you. He trusted you, Tiber. He knew your heart. He believed in you. He knew that you would find your way to the right path." He placed his massive hands over her dainty fingers. "And you did."

Tiber sniffled. "I did, thanks to the support from the Jungle tribe."

CHAPTER 20

The full moon rose in the clear midnight blue sky. Sita's hair gently blew in the subtle breeze. This was her first time in the Beach tribe. It was stunning. The day spent with Nahal was a blur.

"Where did the day go?" Nahal chuckled.

"It went way too fast!"

"Did you enjoy yourself?" The pair were walking on the rocks, trying to get a good view of the stilling ocean waters.

"I did." Sita lost her balance a bit. She flailed her arms to recover. Nahal quickly grabbed her hand to keep her from falling.

"Easy, you may want to take your boots off. The mink fur on these slick rocks doesn't work too well."

She passed him her boots. "I can see that."

They found a spot to sit and watch the water. A comforting silence shrouded them.

"Now I have so many questions," Sita whispered.

"Really? Go ahead, I'm ready."

"This festival is so beautiful. How come you hadn't settled down before this season? I mean, look at this!"

"It wasn't really on my mind. My father made me go to my first festival. I wasn't open to the idea of it. Honestly, my mind has been consumed with thoughts of how to end the Moon Curse. So much so that I feel like a fraud being here for the festival."

"What do you mean?"

"Most of the sister tribes don't understand the Moon Curse. So we come here looking for mates, and our tribe has its own set of rules. So when the Beach or Jungle tribes choose a mate from another tribe, they can choose which tribe will be their home residence. We can't because our numbers are too small. If a man or woman chooses a mate from a different tribe, both parties are forced to join the Tribe of Snow and Ice. Also, a two-day festival is not enough time to get to know someone and explain a curse to them. So the curse gets explained as they transition to our tribe."

"So we have been tricking people that come from our sister tribes?"

"Yes, we have. I know it doesn't apply to me because I'm not supposed to have children. But it's principal. If we could get rid of the curse, literally *everything* would be better for us. Listen to me; do you think someone would want to spend the festival hearing me go on about tribe issues?"

"So, where does Neptune fall into all of this?"

"I had a feeling you were going to ask." Nahal smiled. "Neptune is powerful. He has powerful allies in different territories, including the Firehearts! He established a trade agreement among the Landkeepers, which allowed our tribe to have money and trade with other territories for the first time in hundreds of years! And he's no weakling. His water abilities are so powerful, I don't understand why the other tribes didn't want to fall under his leadership. And for me, he cares about our issues and fixing this curse. He said that he knows what causes the Moon Curse. He needs hands to continue his other operations while he prepares a cure. After all these years, there's light at the end of the tunnel."

"I understand how that sounds promising, but why is the price so steep for failing? The tribesmen were killed, and the whole thing with the Tiber, I'm confused."

"I honestly don't know how the tribesmen were killed. I think the Seer did it when she was trying to escape. But the whole Tiber thing was crazy. Neptune had mentioned that his ally was looking for the Fireheart Legend. I guess Tiber saw the Seer have a vision, and she mentioned the Legend or something, but Tiber thought that if she went above and beyond, Neptune would help save Shasa. The whole situation got out of control. Tiber nearly killed her with the poison. I could not get an antidote, and the Seer ended up being a Storm. It was crazy."

"But why would Neptune retaliate against you guys?"

"Honestly, I wasn't that worried. It was not my issue or my fault. But Neptune doesn't like noncompliance. He's been burned so often that we need to show him that we're loyal. He doesn't have to worry about me, though; I'm loyal to the bitter end. I'll do whatever it takes."

"Nahal, I'm worried that Neptune is manipulating you. He's using your loyalty to your tribe and is abusing it. Not just you, but everyone who works on his behalf."

"Sita, he has no motive to manipulate us! He's one of us! He gets us! He knows the Moon Curse and is not settling for this tragedy to continue! Look, hear me out! At one point, I wasn't as concerned about it. But then Shasa was expecting a baby. My family's bloodline would continue at the expense of that woman's life. And it was unbelievable to me that everyone was so happy. She was happy. Shasa knows that when that child is born, she will die. Yet, she is beaming with happiness and pride. It's absolutely ridiculous to me. We have actually normalized being cursed. It's not just Shasa; it's all the women—as if their life purpose is to die for the title of mother. How can we continue like this? Will there be a Tribe of Snow and Ice in one hundred years from now at the rate we are going? The answer is no. We must do something! Neptune is going to do something about it."

Sita stood in front of Nahal, blocking his view of the ocean. "Nahal, it's a lie! Neptune can't fix the Moon Curse!"

Nahal stood up, his eyes searching hers. "Okay. If he can't, what can you do? You're talking like you can fix it! Do you have a better solution?"

"I don't know, but this isn't right! Nahal, did Neptune kill the chief?"

"I don't know! But why would he kill the chief? I still think Tiber did it, honestly. She got caught and slipped out. Her father probably figured out that she was connected with Neptune, and they had a fatal argument. Do I think she just stabbed him? No, absolutely not. I think it could have been an accident in an argument and struggle. I heard some noises, that's what made me walk in. And she was covered in blood. Also, she did what any guilty person would do—she ran!"

"Nahal, she was probably just scared!"

Suddenly, a loud commotion was heard in the distance. People were fleeing from the direction of the hub of Marina's Beach tribe. People scattered, and tribes were leaving in shifts across the ocean strait.

Nahal grabbed Sita and pushed himself in front of her. "It's Neptune! Stay here. I have to go and see what's going on."

"Nahal, no!" She grabbed his arm, pulling him back. "Nahal, please, this isn't right."

"Remember what I said, whatever it takes, even if it makes me the villain." He pulled himself free and ran toward the ocean water, once calm now crashing against the rocks.

*****

Tiber and Cove were on the beachfront when they heard the commotion. The ocean began to rise high into the sky. "It's Neptune! He is trying to lure you out, Tiber. We must go," Cove shouted as he attempted to drag her away.

Tiber was amazed to see the water lifting to the sky like a giant wall. But she was tired of running and tired of being afraid. He killed her father, an elder, and was threatening the entire Beach tribe to make her bend her knee and bow her head. She was different now; this Tiber only bowed her head to the Universe.

"No, I want to see his face. I'm tired of running from him," Tiber resisted.

"You aren't doing this alone," Cove said.

A massive face made of water appeared from the ocean. "I remember the days of the summer festival." The voice sounded muffled in the water.

Marina and her family hurried to the oceanfront. "Neptune, you are not welcome to disturb the traditional festival," the Chiefess screamed.

"But Marina, are you unaware of a murderer among the tribespeople? We would not want another murder to occur. She hails from the Snow tribe and took the life of her own father. I'm only trying to project the Waterbearers. Her name is—"

"What is in a name, Neptune?" Marina yelled. "There are several people with the same name or variations of names among the tribes. If you are confident that a murderer is here, call her to account before a Moonsayer. Call her to account or leave us in peace!"

"That won't be necessary. Snow tribe girl, I've scoured the tribes for your whereabouts, and I know you are blending in with the tribespeople. But realize that people will continue to die in your place until you admit to your crimes," the voice threatened.

Marina slid gracefully, waving her arms gently to pull water from the ocean. "I will cast you out if you continue to make threats and interfere with peaceful tribe customs!"

Other Waterbearers followed the Chiefess's example. They pulled water from the ocean, trying to reveal Neptune. All the tribes worked together in unison, trying to tug the water away from the figure in the water. However, it was futile; Neptune was too strong.

Through the tumultuous tides of confusion and chaos, Tiber saw her chance. As the power of the water surged from her fingertips, she enveloped herself in a swirling cocoon of waves. This distorted her appearance, rendering her unrecognizable. She surged toward the ocean, desperately trying to pinpoint the source of the voice. She found him, but he was mirroring her cocooning technique. His face was a blur, indistinguishable in the chaos.

"So you came to fight? Do you really think that you're strong enough? Or does your sister also have to die to make you bow to this New World Order?"

Hearing Neptune's threat to her sister's life, Tiber was consumed by a surge of anger, a feeling she had never experienced before. The only thing she could focus on was her father's wish for her to save the tribe. 'You are the new moon, and you will rise,' his words echoed in her mind. The ocean water became her weapon, and she launched herself into an underwater battle with Neptune. They were both cocooned, the water providing them with a steady supply of oxygen. Neptune tried to wrest control of the water, leaving her gasping for breath. But Tiber felt a surge of power. She manipulated the water in a swirling motion, using the waves as both her offense and her defense. Neptune was undeniably powerful; the Tribe of Snow and Ice marked his precision, yet he had the resourcefulness of the Jungle tribe and the grace and flexibility of the Beach tribe. She would have thought he was a water god if she didn't know better.

They continued this elaborate underwater attack. Tiber knew that she could not hold up against Neptune much longer. She had grown more assertive in the past few weeks, but not enough to topple anyone with this much proficiency. She had to fall back. The only downside was that Neptune noticed this. Tiber tried to swim closer to the surface, only to be snatched back down with a water whip. The speed at which he dragged her back to the bottom nearly ruptured her eardrums. They had been underwater for several minutes. The cocoon which encased her was severely damaged. Water flooded the cocoon, so she had to get to the surface.

Neptune was fully aware of her need to reach the surface. "Did you really think you could be victorious over me?"

Tiber began inhaling water, and her vision began to haze. She wasn't afraid to die. Chelan had the decree, and the tribe would be fine. She completed her father's last mission to the best of her ability. She was ready to succumb to this end. To die was a fair punishment for all the things she'd done and everyone who had had to suffer. Tiber was at peace. She learned to believe and repent. She felt cleansed of her wrongdoings.

Her eyes gazed up at the moon, fragmented by the waves of water, for the last time. It was wonderful.

If my end means new beginnings, take me now. Take my life, break this curse. Universe, save them. Like her vision, her consciousness began to go dark.

As life slipped away, she felt her head break through the surface. She inhaled. There was an incredible surge of power. The tides began to grow wide with rapid waves. The Waterbearers on the beach started to fall back. Tiber saw Nahal in the water. He had to be looking for Neptune! Fury filled her heart. Suddenly, she was snatched back underwater.

"Nahal!" Sita cried out to him.

"Sita, stay back; I have to help Neptune! I must prove my loyalty."

"No!" Sita ran into the ocean before propelling herself upward in a tight water spiral. Nahal attempted to pull the water from the spiral to no avail.

"It's no use, Nahal. You may be the stronger Waterbearer, but I'm more spiritual than you. On a full moon like tonight, I'm at the peak of my power."

She thought he would look at her with disdain; however, there was only awe. It was almost as if he didn't care that he was no longer the stronger Waterbearer.

Nahal raised his hands high, fingers intertwining as he propelled himself up in a spiral of water. They were eye to eye. "So what are we to do about this predicament?"

Sita's eyes were glassy, "How can you ask me to sit back and watch people get hurt? Neptune is hurting people, Nahal. What's the point of saving our tribe if we destroy our sister tribes?"

"Neptune will—"

"I'm willing to do whatever it takes to keep you from destroying yourself, even if that makes me the villain of your story." Within seconds, Sita encased Nahal in a thick ice cube as her declaration distracted him. No longer in control of his abilities, the ice block containing Nahal collapsed from the top of the spiraling water into the ocean. With tears in her eyes, she dove into the water and pushed the frozen Nahal upward and onto the edge of the beach.

Meanwhile, Tiber had emerged from the ocean, lifting the water into massive walls. The Waterbearers on the beach ran for cover. Twisting her hands in a swirling motion, the waves crashed and crashed over and over again. She flooded the beach with rage and fury. She was completely out of control.

"Tiber, stop!" A woman on a winged creature called out to her. "Tiber, you have to stop. Look at them!" Tiber's navy-blue eyes were met with the piercing gaze of the silver-eyed Windmaster.

Tiber felt as if her mind was being shaken free from a heavy fog, "Aqila," she whispered.

"Yes, it's me! I'm here for you, Tiber, but you have to stop." Aqila gently turned Tiber's face to the beachfront.

It was a mess. The festival was ruined. Everyone was huddled, holding onto each other. She was beginning to feel like herself, and her powers were losing momentum. Her feet gracefully touched the sand. Aqila followed her. Looking to the Windmaster with tears in her eyes. "I could have killed all of them! I—I don't know what happened to me. How did I suddenly become powerful like that? I was never taught any of those moves. No, it can't be. I—" She ran into the ocean.

"Tiber! It's okay! You can't run from it!" Aqila called to her.

Cove ran toward Aqila, grabbed her arm, and shook her violently. "What just happened? Why is she leaving?"

"Release me! Don't you realize what she is?" Aqila yelled.

"Everyone, listen!" Marina called everyone's attention. "What happened is not as important as what we have been saved from. Neptune attacked us, and we all rallied together in a grand display of unity. United, we were unbreakable.

"One among us was willing to battle with the beast on behalf of all of us. What just happened? We don't know. Maybe it is not for us to understand. Let gratitude fill our hearts instead of questions. Everyone is allowed to stay in the Beach tribe, and we will grandly resume the festival tomorrow. Tonight, let's reflect on our unity."

Cove and Aqila looked puzzled at what Chiefess Marina said.

The Chiefess walked over to them. "Please don't argue. Leave things with Tiber to me."

"Thank you, Chiefess. I am here to assist Tiber. She needs to return to her tribe. It's a matter of great importance."

"Thank you, Aqila. Rest assured that Tiber will meet you at the Tribe of Snow and Ice." Marina smiled at them.

CHAPTER 21

Tiber ran into the ocean as far as she could before returning to the Beach tribe. She cocooned herself underwater, desperate to find Neptune. She found it perplexing that there were no signs of him. It was as if he had disappeared into thin air, which Tiber knew was impossible. She searched for nearly an hour, and finally, she gave up.

She made it to the rocky cliffs near the beach, far away from the hub of the tribe. It seemed like the life of the evening had deserted everyone, and it was quiet. Never had such stillness consumed a Waterbearer tribe at night. Tiber hugged her knees. She was confused. She felt like she didn't know who she was anymore. *How did Aqila know to come? How did she know what to say?*

"How does it feel to have everything you wanted?"

Tiber turned her back, "This is nothing I wanted. You should know that, Marina."

"You could not escape the inevitable."

Tears fell down Tiber's face at the sudden realization. "You knew. You knew the entire time. Why didn't you tell me?"

"It wasn't my place to tell, Tiber. Please try to understand me. I told you before that your father entrusted me with great secrets. We were friends for a long time. There is so much that you don't know. You were born two weeks late. After your tribe medic could not induce the birth, your father requested my audience. I hurried and tried what I knew, to no avail.

"The lunar eclipse was drawing near. Eventually, you were born during the peak of the eclipse. I delivered you myself. Your tribe was praying to spirits during the eclipse, and your parents were anxious. Your mother's dying wish was that we protect you from those who wished you harm. Your tribe doesn't believe in the Universe or Legends. The last Legend was detrimental to your tribe.

"Your father was afraid that you would be sacrificed. He told everyone that you were born early the next morning, and they believed it. He did everything he could to protect you, doing all he could to honor your mother's final wish."

"I can't be a Legend . . . I just can't be." Tiber groaned.

"All Legends have different beginnings, Tiber. Cyra was the daughter of a wealthy merchant. Basir was the son of a scholar. Aenon was a Moonsayer and the son of a fisherman. Ila was an orphan. We don't choose our beginnings, but we can choose where we end up. I must go back, clean up, and prepare for the second day of the festival. I won't allow our traditions to be disrupted. We will not cower in fear because Neptune made an appearance. Regardless of what you decide to do, I'll be on your side."

Tiber watched as Marina's shadow disappeared into the night. Desiring nothing more than to be alone, she rolled her eyes at hearing gentle footsteps approaching.

"How are you holding up?"

"Go away, Aqila. I want to be alone right now."

"Being a Legend isn't easy, and it may not even be what you wanted. But why argue with destiny?" the

Windmaster asked, stretching out on the rocky cliff, looking relaxed.

"You didn't feel it. It was like I was being consumed. For a moment, I couldn't tell the difference between myself and the power. I wanted Neptune's head so badly that I almost destroyed everything that had been good to me. I don't want to ever feel that again."

"There is no difference between you and the power anymore. That's what you must realize. You have everything you will ever need to be successful."

"My father knew the whole time. He never got a chance to see me become a woman or figure out what I wanted to do with my life. It's an empty feeling, and I feel unworthy. I still can't believe that you're here. I mean, I almost killed you."

"And I almost killed you. I, too, felt an incredible surge unlike anything I had ever experienced. I thought I was making a storm like I had many times before. However, that time, it was different. Techniques that I hadn't remembered ever learning, I had mastered. I was seconds away from killing you. But the Universe sent me a reminder that what I was about to do was not the Windmaster way."

"You're a—"

"Yes, I am. Who would have thought when I was your captive, that in two months, this would be where we'd be sitting? But the Universe knows best. I would not have realized the truth about myself if I had not gone through that experience. You would not have realized who you are if you hadn't given the Universe a chance. Even though it was a rough path, we both needed the resulting outcome. I needed the trial. You needed the faith. Now, we are here."

"Do you think that we can stop Neptune and Agni?"

"I believe, with the guidance and power of the Universe, that we have the potential to bring much-needed peace to our people and the world."

"But, the stories—what if we turn out like the last Legends?"

"We won't. Our predecessors taught us what division creates—nothing but a world of chaos, leaving a world of suffering in its wake. It is up to us to fix what they could not. If we don't, there won't be a world to enjoy."

"What should I do?"

"First, go to your friends. You may have scared some of the Waterbearers, but everyone was grateful that you tried to battle Neptune. The friendships you made weren't severed tonight. So please don't cut them off. Together, you'll have the support you need to overcome any trial you may face. Reconnect with them tonight. Tomorrow, I'm going to your tribe, and your name will be cleared," Aqila advised.

Tiber wanted to thank her for taking the time to talk to her, but when she turned to speak, Aqila was already gone. Tiber smiled. Who would have thought that she would have ever considered Aqila as her friend?

She took her time over the rocks and walked on the lonely beachfront. Marina cleaned up rather quickly. The beach looked lovely, and one would never have suspected that any fighting took place there. As she strolled along, gathering her thoughts, she saw a lonely figure sitting in the water.

As she walked closer, Tiber realized it was Cove sitting, staring at the moon. "Are you okay?"

He chuckled, never looking up at her. "Yeah, I guess I should be asking you that."

"I'm better now. I was scared."

"I was, too. I felt so much guilt and regret all at once. I promised I would keep you safe and have your back. I petitioned so hard for you to trust me."

"You did keep me safe, and you had my back and . . . I do trust you with my life. You took me in when I had nowhere to go. You put your alliances on the line to help me. You brought Aqila in on my behalf. You have done so much for me. You believed in me when I didn't believe in myself. Please, don't feel guilty."

"Why did you run?"

"When Aqila started talking to me, it was like being snapped out of a trance. I looked and saw the disquiet in everyone's eyes. It reminded me of the night my father was murdered. Everyone looked at me like I was a criminal. I ran for my life then, and I found myself doing the same again. I was afraid of being shunned, hated, and hunted with a bounty over my head." Tiber cried.

"Shh, I'm still here. I didn't run then, and I'm not running now. I just wanted to help you. I didn't know how, and not being able to fight beside you was killing me." With wet hands, Cove wiped her tears. "You're soaked. Let's go back to the hub. Then we can get some dry clothes." The pair walked through the moonlight into the hub of Marina's tribe.

CHAPTER 22

Sita hugged the ice that covered Nahal. He looked so calm and peaceful.

"I'm sorry, Nahal. I had to do something. You were only going to self-destruct. I wish I could make you see what I see. Neptune isn't going to save us; he doesn't know how. I believe that the moon that cursed us can also save us, but I'm not sure how. I'm sorry," Sita sobbed. She missed Nahal. She didn't know what to do. She just knew that Neptune had to be stopped, and Nahal would die before he let that happen.

"Is everything okay over here?" a raspy voice called out to her.

Sita wiped her eyes and stood up. "You're a Windmaster!" Sita strained her neck to look up at Aqila.

"Nahal's in ice?"

"How do you know Nahal?"

"I'm Aqila the Seer."

"I see. I'm Sita of the Tribe of Snow and Ice. This is called Forever Ice. Only the one who encased him can free him. I'm not sure who to ask for help."

Aqila raised her brow. "You don't say? Well, you may want to join the other Waterbearers. I can bring Nahal back to your tribe."

"Th—thank you." Sita lowered her head and walked away.

"One thing after another." Aqila groaned. She sighed as she saw Talon's broad feathered back. She was exhausted, but her blood was on fire. She scoured her soul for peace but found none. She was supposed to attend a meeting here, but instead, she found Tiber tapping into her Legendary power.

How did I miss the signs before?

She sighed again. All of her doubts came crashing into her thoughts. She knew precisely what Tiber meant when she expressed feelings of unworthiness. Aqila wrestled with the same feeling every time she missed a sign, the sense that she would never be half the Seer Zeroun was.

Lost in thought, she was somewhat startled when she heard her name. When she turned around, she saw Kavi dismounting Sterling, but he was not alone. She could hear wings flapping above them.

"Were you tailed?" she asked, getting into a defensive stance.

"No, I had to bring an ally along. What's wrong?"

"An ally?"

"Yes, I intend to introduce you. Aqila, what's wrong?"

"Nothing."

"Aqila, talk to me," he whispered, concern evident in his gray eyes.

"Why are you so late? This is unlike you."

"My apologies. My companion held me up." He signaled upward. Kavi's apparent ally flew down. The dasher was not clear in the moonlight. "Aqila, this is Haneul."

"The man that's been tailing me? Kavi, what are you doing?"

"Allow me to explain." Haneul walked toward her, his long braid gliding behind him. "Kavi employed me to ensure your safety. Then I came across some information on Neptune. When I reported back to him, the plans changed. I did not intend for us to scuffle the other day, but I urgently needed to report my findings to Kavi."

Aqila was furious. She closed her eyes and clenched her fists around Talon's reins.

"Haneul, could you give us a minute?" Kavi sighed.

"Yeah. Just come and get me when you're ready." Kavi watched Haneul mount and fly off before turning to Aqila.

"What's wrong? Why are you so upset?"

"Why am I upset? When did you start having someone follow me around? Did you forget that I work with highly confidential information? You don't think I can do my job anymore?"

"Aqila, Aqila, take it easy, please." He touched her shoulders, only for her to turn her back on him. "I didn't think that this would upset you. If I thought you'd be upset, I would not have done it . . . you know that. You know my heart. I just wanted to protect you. It's been on my mind for a long time—how to protect you when you're a Seer and I'm ruling Kashmala. It is always on my mind. Haneul just happened to feel like the right answer. He proposed making a select team that could spot you when you're traveling far away. I was still playing around with the idea.

"Then, when Tiber captured you, I regretted not acting sooner. That's how the Red Wing was formed. Haneul just happened to intercept a message from Agni to Neptune while you were away. That's when we came up with the idea for Haneul to go to Neptune and lead him to believe that we have some Windmasters who want to join their effort."

"I just wished we had talked about this first. I mean, I thought that someone intended to do me or Jai harm. Why didn't you tell me?"

"I'm sorry. I should not have let so much go unsaid between us. I intended to talk to you about the subject, but we have been bogged down. We are always incredibly busy with something, and we barely have time to talk. But, Aqila," he clasped her hands, "my silver-eyed queen, you do know that I love you. I'm not perfect, but I'd never do anything to hurt you intentionally. You're the owner of my heart. Your brows are like bows, your lashes are arrows, and every time you look at me, I can't help but surrender."

Aqila stood on her tiptoes and kissed Kavi's cheek. "I love you, too. I know you'd never hurt me. Forgive me for being harsh with you."

"Love, it's in the past . . . Aqila, you've been uneasy. I know something else is bothering you, and my revelation didn't help. What's wrong? It burdens my heart to feel like I can't ease your mind."

Aqila huffed and wiped her eyes but found herself crying in Kavi's arms. He gently stroked her hair to calm her. "My silver-eyed baby, talk to me."

"I'm the worst Seer ever! I missed everything, and I don't know why. I've never been so frustrated. Something crazy happened at this festival that I should have seen coming. I wish Zeroun were here to help me. I don't feel ready to be a Seer without him."

"I can't imagine how hectic things have been for you these past couple of months. I understand now that asking Haneul to spot you made you feel like you weren't doing your job well. Aqila, you're a wonderful Seer. Even though the title is yours now, you're still learning, and that's perfectly all right. We are students in life until the day we die. It is a blessing to wake up every day knowing there is something new to learn. You're so incredibly hard on yourself. Just because you have the sight doesn't mean you must change everything. That's why everyone has a destiny. Maybe that's why we have four Legends. The weight of everything, good or bad, doesn't rest in the hands of one person. Your destiny is grand, and you are ready. How do I know? Zeroun would not have left this world without preparing you to do your best."

"Thank you. I got worked up for nothing."

Kavi kissed her hand. "No, you just forgot how amazing you are, and it is my job to remind you when you forget." The pair embraced and looked into each other's eyes.

"Can we negotiate some of the terms of this Red Wing alliance, maybe over the gala?"

"Why don't we let it wait until after the gala? This weekend, I think we should take some time to relax and casually catch up since we've been so busy."

Aqila smiled. "I agree. Let's get Haneul so we can unravel some of these mysteries about Agni and Neptune."

Kavi went to get Haneul, and Aqila let out a sigh of relief. Kavi was right. Just because she was a full Seer didn't mean she wasn't human. She was still getting used to her new responsibilities as a Seer and Legend. Voicing her fears cleared her mind's eye. For the first time in a few days, she felt something coming.

Your fiancé is right; don't be hard on yourself. Have faith in your unique abilities. Every Seer has its own unique way of reading the sight. We are always with you. Emet's voice came clearly.

Aqila wondered how she could hear him so clearly when he was the first Seer but could not hear the later Seers.

The mind's eye is strong; it will call for help from the Seer best equipped to answer. You and I are much alike. I was the first Seer, and you are the first Legend Seer. Our plights are very similar. We are all here with you.

Kavi and Haneul returned. "Thank you for looking out for me, Haneul. I admit I was surprised, but I am thankful that Kavi and I can call you our ally."

"I'm honored to serve any way I can. Let me provide you with the details I have thus far."

CHAPTER 23

Tiber lay on Mika's back and looked up at the stars. She reflected on Aqila's words and laughed to herself when she remembered how she used to hate hearing Aqila talk. Now, she values every word that falls from her lips. She reflected on her father. It was all starting to make sense. He asked her to save the tribe because he knew that she could. He was worried about the attack because she was a Legend. He tried to keep Neptune from his tribe to protect her, even though they shared similar values. He indeed did his best for her and Shasa. Tiber felt peace. She had nearly forgotten what that felt like. She had looked for her life's purpose for a long time and finally found her place, along with an unquenchable thirst for change and adventure. Her heart longed for her father. She just wanted to tell him that she understood now, had his back, and would preserve his legacy. Everything would be all right.

The warm heat from the sun began to sting Tiber's eyelids. She couldn't recall falling asleep. When she opened her eyes fully, she saw Aqila sprinkling sand over her.

"Stop it. You're going to get sand in my eyes!" Tiber picked up a fist full of sand and tossed it at her.

The Windmaster used a gentle wind wisp to deflect the half-hearted attack. "I was only trying to wake you up." She chuckled. "Let's go. Are you ready to meet with your tribe so we can set the record straight?"

Tiber looked around, "What about Cove?"

"What about him? He had to go back to his tribe. He felt the need to settle them after the Neptune attack. Come on." Aqila mounted her dasher and flew off. Tiber took a little time to wash up before riding Mika into Jungle tribe territory. Her beautiful panther fit perfectly with the jungle scene. Tiber wondered if the Tribe of Snow and Ice could ever truly be home to her again. *What is my purpose as a Legend? I surely cannot stay in my tribe all the time. Neptune knows about me. Will staying in my tribe bring danger to my people?* Sadness began to fill her heart. Would she ever be able to call any place home?

She rode by the Jungle tribe. Instinctively, she called for Mika to stop. Tiber's navy-blue eyes took in the scene. The river, the vines, and the thick, lush canopy of the trees sang to her. Looking up to the sky, a part of her did not want to leave. She saw the women washing by the river and heard the squeals of young children playing. She would miss this tribe. She saw Cove walk through the hub on the way back to his tent. Tiber caught herself wanting to call out to him. But she did not. The Universe knew what was meant to be. The truth was that she was a danger to all of the Waterbearer tribes. How could she put his tribe in danger when he had given her so much?

I'm sorry, Cove. We won't be seeing each other again. I hope you find eternal peace and happiness. The Universe knows I will never forget you. I can't change what I'm destined to be, but I would never jeopardize everything you've built and maintained. I knew that last night was goodbye. I'm sorry I wasn't brave enough to say it to your face.

With a heavy heart, she told Mika to continue. Tears streamed down her face. She whispered, "Great love requires great sacrifice."

It took her nearly an hour to meet Aqila. "Are you ready to go?" she asked.

"Yes, I'm ready," Tiber replied.

Sita ran to her. "I'm so glad you've returned. Things can go back to normal now."

They carefully proceeded up the mountain. Talon carried Nahal, the ice block in his talons, up the mountain. When Aqila landed, followed by Sita and Chelan, a great commotion was heard in the tribe.

A tall, slim, cerulean-eyed man greeted them, "Sita and Chelan, what is the meaning of this? Where are our tribespeople? What is this Windmaster doing here?"

The Tribe of Snow and Ice gathered around the trio. "I am Aqila the Seer. I am here on urgent business to report a massive plot to destroy this tribe. There is a sinister traitor among you. He goes by the name of Neptune. Last night, he attempted to kill Waterbearers as they enjoyed the summer festival. With the sight given to me by the Stars themselves, I've seen that some of your tribe support Neptune. The sight showed me that Neptune killed your chief and conveniently framed his daughter for the crime. However, I have managed to hold one of Neptune's avid supporters. It was essential to prevent this already small tribe from experiencing any fatalities. Here he is. Talon, bring him forth." The dasher dropped the ice block containing Nahal.

The tribe gasped. The cerulean-eyed man snatched Aqila by her clothes and glared upward, for she was much taller than him. "You're a liar! You're a Windmaster. You could not have done this—"

Sita interrupted, "The Windmaster bears the truth."

"It can't be! Free my son!" Mahak was furious.

"I cannot, like you said, I am only a Windmaster. How could I free him? Mahak, this ice is so thick that only the one who did this to him can free him. It's an ancient technique known as Forever Ice. Seeing that Neptune is so powerful, I think you should reconsider your alliance with him if you want your son back."

"Father, you're with Neptune?" Muraco asked, stepping in front of Shasa.

"I don't have to answer any of these questions."

"You do if your tribe demands answers," an elder shouted.

"What are you talking about? Who's making demands? Do you not realize who's been handling this tribe? Apparently not! Trade has picked up, we have money, and the number of the tribe has begun to stabilize. You all have me to thank for that. The Neptune that I know has provided us with supplies and medicines that have benefitted us for nearly twenty years. You dare accuse me of destroying our home and people. Aqila, if you are a real Seer, who is Neptune?"

"Tribe of Snow and Ice, I can only tell you what the Stars have blessed me to see. The sight has said, 'The sea has one set of eyes but two faces.' The Stars did not give me a name. Furthermore, Tiber is cleared of all accusations. And the decree of this tribe has been found."

After Aqila spoke, Chelan gave the decree to Mahak.

He grabbed it from his hands. "It's authentic. It has the snowflake seal of our tribe. It reads: To the Tribe of Snow and Ice. This is the decree of Chief Dalit. The successor of this tribe has shown great consideration for his tribe's brothers and sisters. He will lead the tribe with love and dignity and allow the Tribe of Snow and Ice to support the brotherhood of the Waterbearers. Welcome Chief Muraco in a grand fashion. Trust in him and support his leadership. Fallen star, Chief Dalit."

The tribe cheered as Muraco appeared shocked to be named chief. Mahak bowed his head. "Congratulations, son."

Muraco ignored his father's congratulations and spoke to the tribe, "Tribe of Snow and Ice, I am honored to be your Chief. I wish it were under better circumstances, but Fallen Star Dalit would have wanted us to keep moving forward. Tiber is cleared of suspicions of murder, for Aqila, the Seer, has exonerated her. My council and I will investigate the claims of Neptune, and we will not stand for his treason and crimes against us or our fellow Waterbearers."

The tribe cheered and began to scatter. "Where are they going?" Sita asked.

Shasa took a deep breath. "To prepare for the Rising Star ceremony in honor of our new chief. Where's Tiber?"

Chelan and Sita looked around. "I don't know. I thought she was coming to join us."

Aqila closed her eyes. "She will come when she is ready. A lot has happened in the past months, and it is only her story to tell."

Shasa looked on in sadness as she slowly walked back to her tent. Chelan and Sita followed behind her.

Mahak cleared his throat. "Aqila, I am prepared to answer any questions you have. I don't want my tribe to feel I am a threat to them in any possible way."

"If Chief Muraco will allow us a moment for questioning."

"Of course, Aqila. Should I come too?"

"Not at all. You should stay with your tribe's customs and console your wife. If anything else is needed, I will request it."

Mahak motioned for Aqila to follow him, and he led her to his tent. "We should talk inside."

"Talon, stay out here. We will be leaving shortly." She followed Mahak inside the rather large tent.

"I can never repay you for your expert judgment." Mahak sighed.

"The truth, Mahak. That is the only form of repayment that I want from you."

"What else can I say? I am not an enemy of the Waterbearer tribes. I am an advocate for my tribe and my people. I work only to bring equality, and my track record reflects that. I will admit, however, that I am perplexed by your accusations in the murder of the chief—I am Neptune."

"I know. What are your dealings with Agni?"

"I'm at a loss. I don't know what you are talking about."

"Your ally?"

"Aqila, I give you my word. I do not know any Agni. My only alliances are within the Waterbearer tribes, and I have a lucrative venture in Theyra."

"What kind of venture?"

"I am funding a manufacturing initiative in Theyra."

"Manufacturing in Theyra? What are they making?"

"Materials to be used for infrastructure, processing metals, and alloys for trading purposes, as well as irrigation and jewelry. They are even replicating weapons."

"Why weapons?"

"Weapons weren't my idea. It was theirs. They would not agree to the collaboration unless they could produce the necessary arms for the war. It makes sense. They are the underdogs. Try to understand. Twenty years ago, this tribe consisted of less than fifty people. The Moon Curse is responsible for our pitiful population. Our tribe could not attract mates during the summer festival because of the curse.

"Chief Dalit was grieving over the death of his first wife, and as his council, I had to do something about it. Our tribe had to have something to offer. No longer could we continue to be a financially broke and physically needy tribe. I made a deal with Marina. I would sell her a valuable product from our tribe, something that most of our tribe people don't even know is here. I showed it to her. She loved it and begged to have it. I sell this product to her at a price that is four times the cost to produce.

"Once I stabilized our finances, I pursued trading for the tribe. I used a different name in trading. It was necessary due to my controversial bloodline. I am not involved in anything else. I know of no crimes or betrayals, and definitely, I know no one named Agni."

Aqila was perplexed. "What do you mean by controversial bloodline?"

"I'm the son of Jocasta, the great-granddaughter of Queen Avala and Legend Aenon—known to the world as the Queen of Blood and Ice and the Lame Legend."

WAR ON THE HOME FRONT

The smell of sand tickled Boaz's nose. The sun was setting on the horizon. His sage green eyes watched as the sun's rays began to disappear. The dusky sky would have been a peaceful scene if it wasn't for the feverish screams and cries. The sounds were deafening, the earth began rumbling. Landkeepers at war made the earth shake. Boaz frowned, he hated war.

A gentle hand touched his shoulder. The soft aroma of jasmine danced in his nostrils. Someone sat beside him and laid their head on his shoulder.

"What's on your mind, son?"

"I should be fixing this . . . I should have been fixing this. I just don't know how."

"The stars will guide your path. You are enough as you are." His mother smiled. Her bright green eyes looked angelic complimenting her velvety brown skin.

He sighed as the smell of blood pierced the air. Boaz hung his head.

"Endure, Boaz." His mother squeezed his hand.

"I will to the best that I can. We have to end this war. So much is happening in the other nations and territories, that if we don't get it together, we won't survive."

"We are Landkeepers, we don't like change. The road will be hard, but not impossible. We had to move to the outskirts of Theyra right after we were married. We knew that the best way to raise our family in safety."

An anxious silence came between them. Boaz looked at his mother from the side of his eye. She was looking straight ahead at the violence, unflinching.

This is all she has ever known.

His heart ached. He parted his lips to say the words he should have said long ago. Words that part of his still wonders if he had the courage to say.

Suddenly, the truth fell from his lips, "I'm leaving the desert. I won't return until Theyra is a better place. And if I never return, please know that I gave everything I had and died trying."

She never looked at him. Boaz watched as her lips quivered for a brief moment. She sighed deeply before turning to him. She cupped his face in her hands. Her bright green eyes were glassy as she mustered a smile. "We understand that this is something you have to do. The stars speak to you. I trust them to take you to your destiny . . . and bring you back home to us—to me."

Her hand slid to his shoulder as she dropped her head. Boaz gently moved her hand and watched as it fell limp at her side. He forced himself to walk away. As he approached his sand raft, he looked back at his mother.

"Mom, I love you."

She perked at hearing his words. With a small smile she replied, "I love you more."

Boaz imprinted her expression in his mind. It may very well be the last time he saw her face. Guilt and pain wore heavily on his shoulders as he rode his raft through the desert. That was the hardest thing he had ever done. He wasn't intending on saying goodbye to his family. Boaz didn't expect for his mother to come outside. His eyes became glassy at the possibility that he would never see his family again.

I never told them who I am.

His mother's words echoed in his mind, *Endure, Boaz.*

Basir ran his hand through his silver hair nearly pulling it from his scalp. Cyra could sense his raging frustration. She could understand, her frustration was reaching its peak as well. They were in Theyra, in the library run by sages of varying ages.

"So, what you are telling us is that traumatic events can trigger Giftless people to have limited access to their abilities?" Basir asked.

An elderly man with pale green eyes nodded his head. "It's possible, however, it's not common. I wish I could tell you more regarding the eclipse. What I do know, is that if the person in question is a Fireheart, a solar eclipse will maximize their power."

Basir eyed Cyra carefully. "Well, thank you for your time. I'd like to visit again at a later date to do some more research on the topic."

The elder chuckled. "Of course! Master Basir, your scholarly pursuits are most admirable. Before you leave, I'm afraid I must ask if there is a specific person in question."

"N-No, not at all." Cyra blurted. Her golden eyes widened.

"If it that happened to be the case, it's your duty as Legends to inform us," the elder reminded them.

Basir rolled his gray eyes. "You've been most helpful." He dragged Cyra out of the library. When they were a suitable distance away, he huffed. "Now we're lying to sages."

"What could I say? They were on to me! I just wish we could have gotten more from them. I just thought they would have had more information."

"It's the Giftless we are talking about. We knew that whatever we came across was going to be limited. I'm not surprised by the outcome. We learned enough. Either way, we are facing a big problem. Based on Zeroun's vision solar eclipses will awaken her abilities in full force. Also, if I'm interpreting this right, only lightning can stop her. So only you can stop her. I'll back you as best as I can—"

"I know it's my battle. It's just, she's my daughter. I see the best and worst of Aenon and myself in her. Basir, I've already lost a daughter. The pain, there's nothing like it. I can't imagine losing another child, my last child. I failed them."

"Cyra, you did the best you could do by yourself. Now, am I allowed to add my unsavory commentary on the situation?"

"You can't help it. Go on."

"Well, Soleil has a following. Every Fireheart who believes that you and Aenon are reason the world is at war supports her. Eventually, at least among the Firehearts, it will be you versus her. Now, Soleil knows this, too. She is going to take advantage of the eclipse. You should too. It will be a battle in the sky. I can control the wind, you control the lightning."

Cyra wiped her eyes free from tears. "The eclipse is a few weeks away. What do you suggest I do?"

Basir shook his head frantically. "You have to do something about this war. The Firehearts and Waterbearers need a ceasefire. I'm working to get things under control with the Windmasters and Landkeepers. But if you could quell the violence, that could get more supporters on your side."

"I tried, Basir, they don't trust me anymore. Avala told the Waterbearer tribes that I killed Aenon. Then she died."

"I will go to the Waterbearer tribes. I will talk to Kai of the Beach tribe and Pavati of the Jungle tribe."

"Kai was Aenon's best friend. Aenon was from the Beach tribe. I don't think he will listen. You may have a better chance with Pavati, she didn't know Aenon well. She was quite young when we visited the Jungle tribe."

"I intend on speaking to both of them. At the end of the day, it was a horrible accident. Avala wanted to kill you. Aenon got in the way. Kai deserves to know the truth. Aenon's people deserve to know the truth. Regardless of what happened between you two, he was a good man. I hate hearing people curse his name. He made his mistakes, but he was not a lame Legend. Leave the tribes to me."

"I will go to Pyroc."

Cyra opened her golden eyes, her palms were growing sweaty. She looked around at the maroon painted walls adorned with golden paintings. One looked oddly familiar. Her hands traced over the volcano and the rocky slopes that is the edge of Pyroc's territory just before the rocky beaches of the Beach tribe.

"It was a great thing that you did that day," a voice called behind her.

Cyra turned around quickly. There was a woman before her. She appeared to be in her early thirties. Her eyes were bright amber with dark purples scales clustered around her eyes. Deep blood red hair done with a braided updo enhanced the woman's natural beauty. Cyra furrowed her brows.

"You looked surprised to see me, General Cyra." The woman smiled.

Cyra bowed deeply. "Forgive me."

"Rise, my Legend. I am DragonLady Anala. The last battle you led, as depicted in that picture, was against the Beach tribe and I was kidnapped. You put the most dangerous maneuvers on hold until I was secured. Much has happened, but I will always be grateful and in debt to you."

"DragonLady Anala, it was my honor to serve in the DragonGuard. I'd do it all over again if I could. That was the highlight of my life."

"Thank you. Now, you have requested my audience. How can I assist?"

"I need help trying to end the violence in the Fireheart territories. We need a ceasefire in this war against the Waterbearers."

"I will consult with Ignacio. However, I have no intention of trying to convince the other territories of anything. I would be open to ending tensions with the Beach tribe. We have been on horrible terms for at least a hundred years. I am willing to negotiate a treaty with them. Extending beyond my reach as a new DragonLady would not be wise. I hope you understand and respect my position."

"Yes, of course. Any assistance is greatly appreciated."

"Pyroc is always aligned with the Fireheart Legend." Suddenly, the heavy golden doors opened. Long blood red hair and sharp amber eyes on a masculine face. His footsteps commanded authority as the jade scales on his face pulsated. The DragonLady nodded. "Commander Ignacio, thank you for gracing us with your esteemed presence."

"Cyra?" He whispered.

The DragonLady cleared her throat. "Commander, our Legend would like for us to attempt to negotiate a treaty with the Beach tribe on her behalf in attempt to slow down this war. I do have another matter to attend to. Please discuss with our Legend and report your decisions back to me. Good day." Anala walked out of the war room with her golden robes trailing behind her.

Ignacio closed the door after the DragonLady left.

Cyra rushed to Ignacio, stopping right as the pair were face to face. "Ignacio, I'm so sorry—"

He silenced her with an embrace. "Bygones are bygones." He took a step back. "It's been a long time. What can I do for you?"

"My daughter is in trouble. She has been using the war to my disadvantage. On the solar eclipse, Soleil will be able to use an unbelievable amount of power—"

"Cyra, this war Soleil is revving up is against you. I've heard rumors, Soleil hates Legends. She blames you for Aenon's death . . . as do a lot of people."

"I didn't kill him. It was Avala and it was an accident. I need help to slow down the war with the Waterbearers."

"It's war, Cyra. I can't make any promises. I will see what Pyroc can do. It would be wise for you to prepare for the eclipse, that is if you plan to survive."

Their gazes met before Cyra lowered her head and headed for the door.

"I'm sorry about Aenon," Ignacio sighed.

"I made a mistake, but I never wanted things to end the way they did . . . It's good to see you again."

He chuckled. "I've missed you too." His eyes followed her wavy hair until he couldn't see her anymore.

www.ingramcontent.com/pod-product-compliance
Lightning Source LLC
Chambersburg PA
CBHW032354310726
48973CB00007B/2014